MW01504523

HER BILLIONAIRE HERO

A FRIENDS TO LOVERS SECOND CHANCE
ROMANCE (IRRESISTIBLE BROTHERS 4)

SCARLETT KING

MICHELLE LOVE

CONTENTS

Made in "The United States" by:

Scarlett King & Michelle Love

© Copyright 2021

ISBN: 978-1-64808-774-5

ALL RIGHTS RESERVED. No part of this publication may be reproduced or transmitted in any form whatsoever, electronic, or mechanical, including photocopying, recording, or by any informational storage or retrieval system without express written, dated and signed permission from the author

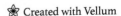 Created with Vellum

BLURB

My dream is about to become a reality: owning my own resort and spa.
All I have to do is build it. That's where she comes in.
The strongest woman I've ever met but also one of the most broken.
She keeps her cards close to the vest, never revealing much about her past.
Divorced, no kids, and with a new career, she's on her way to a new and better life. A life I want to become part of.
Friendship blossoms into much more; the future looks bright for us.
Only it doesn't seem to be in her ex's plans for her to move on. Not with me. Not with anyone.
Secrets from her past threaten to break her further. She needs someone to protect her–to save her.
She needs me. I need her.
Our love is strong. I have to make her see that we need each other; my time to convince her is running out. Some things are too important to wait for.

1

BALDWYN

Letting up off the gas, my stomach churned nervously as I entered Carthage, Texas, with my four younger brothers.

Patton, the second oldest, sat in the passenger side of my Lincoln Navigator, leaning in to look at the ever-slowing speedometer. "What's up, Baldwyn?"

Gripping the steering wheel, I clenched my jaw, unsure of what to say. I shook my head and shrugged my shoulders.

My youngest brother, Stone, spoke up. "He's getting the bubble guts because we're about to meet men we've never met before and use our 'in' as their second cousins to see if we can get a huge business loan."

Cohen, the second youngest brother, nodded. "Yeah, Patton, what's not to understand? I'm grinding my teeth back here." Sitting alone in the third-row seat, he cracked his knuckles as he took a deep breath.

"The worst thing that can happen is that they say no," Warner, the middle brother reminded us all. "We're not destitute, you know. We all still have our jobs. If they say yes, then cool. If not, then no biggie."

"They're billionaires." Cohen punched Warner in the arm then sat back in his seat. "It's just nerve-wracking is all."

Rubbing his shoulder, Warner's narrow eyes caught mine in the rearview mirror. "The Gentrys have only been rich for about a year. I'm sure they haven't been corrupted by the money yet. Plus, their mom told our uncle that they've been looking to invest in something other than the ranch their grandfather left to them. And since we all have extensive experience in the hospitality industry and *most* of us have gotten education to back that experience up, our business venture is pretty much as solid as they come."

Patton took offense right off the bat. "An associate degree *is* education, Warner. My interior design degree has let me in the door of many of Houston's finest spas and resorts. My freelance business is doing quite well. Not many thirty-two-year-old men can say they've done so well in the interior design biz."

Stone chimed in. "Yeah, Warner. Patton's right. My culinary arts degree might only be considered an associate degree, but it's given me access to work with many renowned chefs. I'm not embarrassed by what I've made out of myself at only twenty-four. And I'll be damned if any of these long-lost cousins of ours make me feel inadequate for not having more education."

I had to stop them all before the whole thing disintegrated into a sibling bashing fest. "Look, guys, we're all educated, and all of us have the experience we need to make this spa and resort thing work. Plus, I doubt our cousins have gained any education in the period of only a year. From what Uncle Rob said, his cousin married a man who gave up the money and ranch he stood to inherit. Our cousins grew up without much money at all—hence why they put the word out about wanting to invest in businesses to help out some of the family they never knew."

Cohen smiled proudly. "We've got what it takes to make this work. And I'm sure Tyrell, Jasper, and Cash Gentry will see fit to finance our project. Even if they don't, that's okay. If it's meant to be, it'll be. The most important thing here is that we're going to meet relatives we never knew existed. If nothing else comes of this, we've gained more family. One can never have too many family members."

"You're right," Stone agreed. "Family is more important than money. And we should start out by saying that, Baldwyn. Make sure to let them all know that no matter what they say about the deal, we're still family and always will be."

"Of course I'll start with that." Biting my lip, I chewed it as I turned onto the road that led to Whisper Ranch. "I sort of hate that the first time meeting them, we're asking for money. But what other choice do we have? Uncle Rob said we needed to get out here before the vultures came to take away their money."

We had plenty of relatives who would lie to get their hands on some of our newly rich family members' money. Family members who'd never met any of their relatives. Family members who might be a bit naïve about people they should be able to trust.

Our father's side of the family wasn't exactly made up of the best people in the world. Uncle Rob was an exception—he was completely trustworthy. He had mentioned that the reason behind his cousin running off to get married to the wealthy rancher's son had everything to do with where she'd come from —the wrong side of the tracks. And that was where our father had also come from. Only, Dad had made something out of himself. He'd married a nice woman he met in college and started his life in Houston.

An enormous gated entrance loomed ahead of us and my stomach rumbled. "Shit, this place is really something, isn't it?"

"Sure is," Patton agreed. "But we've got to remember that we're here to meet our family and the other thing is just a passing question."

"Yeah, that's how we'll do this thing. The money isn't everything. The business idea isn't the be-all, end-all. The important thing here is the men we're related to. Family." I reached out to push the button on the keypad I'd stopped next to. "Okay, so here we go. Let's see if they even let us in."

"Welcome to Whisper Ranch," a man greeted us over the intercom. "How can I help you?"

"We're the Nash brothers." I tried to speak with pride, hoping to convey faith to the man on the other end of the speaker. "We're the Gentry brothers' second cousins. We're here from Houston. Our uncle, Robert Nash, said he called to let Tyrell know that we were coming today."

"Oh, yeah. I'll buzz you guys in." The gate buzzed as it opened.

I let out a sigh of relief, but the nerves weren't gone yet. "Here we go, guys. This might be the best day of our lives. Or it might be just mediocre."

Patton grinned as he looked at everyone in the car. "It's gonna be great no matter what. New family—right, guys?"

Everyone agreed as we drove up the long driveway. Cattle ate grass, some horses looked our way, and one of them galloped alongside of the car for a bit before taking off in the other direction.

Stone stared out the window, mesmerized. "A real ranch. I have to admit I hadn't realized it would be like this. It's nice. Grand. Cool."

"I hope they're nice," Cohen said quietly.

"I'm sure they are." I pulled up behind an expensive-looking truck and put the car in park, then shut off the engine. "K. Let's go."

Before we even got out of the car, three men came out a side door of the ranch house and headed toward us. "Hi there, cousins," the tallest of them called out. "Welcome to Whisper Ranch."

"They seem nice," Warner said as we got out. "Hi there. I'm Warner Nash." He extended his hand.

But the tall guy pushed it to the side, then hugged him. "Tyrell Gentry, Warner. And family hug."

"Jasper," the man right behind him said as he took me in for a hug.

Laughing at how nervous I'd been before, I hugged him back. "Nice to meet you, Jasper. I'm Baldwyn."

Patton came around the front of the car, then was hugged by the last brother.

"I'm Cash."

Hugging the man back, my brother smiled. "Patton."

Stone and Cohen stood there, as if waiting for their turns to get hugged. Cash and Jasper grabbed them up as I introduced them.

"Come on inside the house. We've got some sweet tea ready." Tyrell led us inside.

We entered a small alcove with a coatrack full of raincoats and cowboy hats. It was the only stick of furniture in the small space. Wonderful smells wafted through the air as we headed toward what seemed to be the kitchen.

"It smells good in here," I said. "You guys have an awesome place."

"Thanks," Cash said. "We do like it here."

Passing the kitchen, Tyrell led us to a dining area where more than just iced tea waited on a side table. Several platters of finger foods sat along each side of the large dispenser of tea. Jasper gestured to the serving table. "Help yourselves, gentlemen." He grabbed a glass of ice and filled it up with tea then took a small plate and began filling it. "We had lunch a couple of hours ago, but I've got room for more."

None of us could pass up the food and we all loaded our plates before taking seats at the long table. "Thanks, guys." I held up my glass. "And here's to finding long-lost relatives. May all our future years be happy ones."

"Cheers," everyone said as we clanked our glasses.

"How was the trip in from Houston?" Jasper asked.

An hour of light chit-chat followed, making us all a lot more comfortable with each other. It wasn't until now that the time felt right to bring up our business idea.

So, I went for it. "Our Uncle Rob told us that you boys are looking to make some investments."

"We are," Tyrell confirmed. "But before you go any further, let me tell you that we're not going to be handing money out for just anything. We all must agree on the investment. And I'll let you know right now that we rarely agree on much."

Shit.

Shrugging, I knew I had to accept a negative response if they gave us one. "Let's hope you can see the big picture of what we're proposing here." Looking at Warner, I began to give our credentials. "Between Warner, myself, and Cohen, we've got a couple of master's degrees in business and a bachelor's. Stone has a degree in culinary arts and Patton's got one in interior design. We've all been working in the hospitality industry for years now. There's well over a decade of experience between us."

Jasper held up a finger to stop me. "So, your business idea has something to do with the hospitality industry then?"

"It does," Warner answered. "We're interested in the Austin area."

Stone took over. "The diversity in the capital city is why we've chosen that area."

Cash nodded. "There are a lot of people there. But there are a lot of businesses there for you to compete with. What gives your idea the edge it'll need to take some business away from some of the other ones?"

Cohen said, "First, you should know that our idea is a resort and spa."

Carefully, I pulled the short version of our business plan out of my briefcase and handed it to Tyrell. "Here's the business plan. The basics. We do have a detailed plan as well. But it's a hundred and seventy-five pages long, so I thought we'd start with this."

Tyrell looked it over, then handed it to Cash who sat next to him.

Cash took a few more minutes to check it out than his older brother had, before passing it to Jasper.

Jasper's eyebrow cocked as he browsed, and then he looked at me. "You really think you can get people to pay over a thousand bucks a night to stay at this place?"

"It's all-inclusive. That amount covers the room, the meals, the spa treatments, and whatever else they might want. I currently manage one similar to this. I *know* people will pay that price."

"Interesting," Tyrell said as he took out his phone and started tapping away on it. "If you booked even half of the hundred rooms you've got on the plan, then you'd still come out pretty good."

"I'm not sure about the all-inclusive idea," Cash said. "You've got two bars in that plan. People can drink in Texas, Baldwyn. You could go broke giving out unlimited alcohol."

"The fine print is where we take care of that. There are limits. We will not offer buffets or open bars. Our one and only restaurant will offer meals. Our bar will offer up to five free drinks. After that, if our guests wish for more, it will be added to their bill. The same goes for any food they want over their included meals." I wasn't new to this game. I'd done it for years.

"I'm thirty-five now and started working at a Houston resort fresh out of high school. As an errand boy, I learned my way around the place as I went to college and learned how to run the place. I went from one resort to another, gaining experience as I went."

Patton patted me on the back. "Our oldest brother made the industry sound so interesting that we all took jobs at the various hotels, restaurants, and resorts in our city. We all eventually went to college to gain degrees to help us move up. And its paid off. We're all doing very well. And, as you can see, the oldest of us is only thirty-five. Stone's the youngest at twenty-four and he's worked with world-class chefs. We can make this work. And that means you will make even more money if you decide to finance this endeavor."

Jasper's brow furrowed. Tyrell sat back, crossing his arms over his chest. Cash tapped his fingers on the table. None of them wore a frown, which I found promising.

Standing, Tyrell gave me a nod. "Can you give us a minute? We'll be right back."

"Of course." I stood and smiled as they began to leave. "Hey." I wanted to make sure they knew how we all felt. "No matter what you come back here and tell us, we're very glad to have met you and this won't affect the relationships we hope to build with you men, as our cousins. So, don't feel like you have to say yes to us."

Patton stood up next to me. "But don't think we don't want to hear a yes from you."

Stone added, "We can make this work. I have faith in that. But what matters most is that you know you've got family. Family understands the word no. At least some of us do."

Nodding, they left us alone.

We sat in silence until they returned. I honestly had no idea what the verdict would be. But I was ready for anything. Or so I thought.

Sitting down, the three of them looked at us all before Jasper said, "Let's do this, gentlemen."

Stunned, we all sat there looking at the men who sat across the table from us.

Cash said, "We're going to give you all the money you need to make this a success."

I felt the room tilt, then spin. Then a solid clap on my shoulder brought me back to earth.

Cohen stood behind me with an answer for our cousins. "Thank you. We graciously accept your offer. Together, we will make this work for all of us!"

I'm going to be a business owner. I'm going to have my own resort!

2

SLOAN

ONE, TWO, THREE, FOUR, FIVE—DEEP BREATH.

Hands on the steering wheel, stomach in knots, brain on fire —and all because I was about to start my very first job as a structural engineer.

Whispers Resort and Spa would be my premier project— one I prayed would lead to a prestigious career. Proving my ex-husband wrong about women belonging in the engineering field was one of my top goals in life.

Preston Rivers and my father were into some sort of business venture together and Dad brought him to the house for dinner one evening years ago. I was only eighteen. I'd just started as a freshman at the University of Texas in Austin where I'd grown up.

Preston found it hard to hide his interest in me, a thing my father didn't like at all. Who could blame him? The man was his age, after all—twenty-four years my senior.

Preston tried to hammer into my head that I was wasting my time by taking engineering classes in college. He had no trouble letting my dad know that my current goal would never be attainable, and he should make me change majors. Lucky for me, Dad didn't care what I majored in, as long as I went to college.

Preston and I had already begun dating a few months before Dad moved away to Greece to help his company with a start-up there. My father was extremely unhappy about our relationship though. But just like my college major, he kept his nose out of my personal relationships as well. Plus, Preston always seemed to have my best interests at heart and treated my father and me with the utmost respect.

Not that our relationship moved fast enough to freak my father out anyway. It took Preston four years to decide that he wanted to ask me to marry him. I said yes, of course. With my mother out of the picture and not having a soul to claim as my family anywhere near me, I was eager to make one of my own. So, Preston and I became husband and wife only a month after I received my degree.

I was ready to start looking for a job shortly after we returned from Greece where we took our honeymoon and visited my father for a couple of weeks. But Preston nixed the idea, as he thought we'd be starting a family and he wanted me to stay home with our babies. Working away from home wouldn't be in the picture for *his* wife and the mother of *his* children.

When our first anniversary rolled around a few months later, he fully expected me to surprise him with news of a pregnancy. When I wasn't able to tell him the news he sought, he let me know how very disappointed he was with me. Guilt bore down on me like a load of bricks. The one thing he wanted from me I didn't seem able to give him.

Another year came and went with no baby, and then he gave up on that dream altogether. His dream for me changed. Now he wanted me to go back to school—but I needed to change to a degree that made sense for a woman. Accounting was his grand idea.

Since Preston never paid much attention to the things I did, including my classes, I'd pay the tuition with our joint checking account without him ever knowing that I was well on my way to becoming what I wanted to become—a structural engineer, instead of an accountant.

It wasn't until graduation, when I was twenty-seven, that he learned of my deceit. And that was the beginning of the end of our five-year marriage. Only a couple of months after I had earned my degree and found a job as an apprentice engineer at a construction company, Preston told me something that shook me to my very core.

He'd had an affair with my mother for two years. I'd been ten years old when it started. It only ended when she went missing a couple of years later. And what was worse, my father had found out about the affair when the authorities told him about Preston Rivers' role in my mother's life. Yet, he'd never told me a thing. Not even when he'd brought Preston home that fateful evening years later.

So, of course, I called Dad before I let Preston go on with his story. "Honey, he had no idea that your mother was married or had a child. I saw no reason to doubt his word. And I saw no reason to bring that up to you—even when you began dating him. I figured that was his place to tell you a thing like that. I'm sorry if that hurt you. But the past is the past and there's nothing we can do about it now. Your mom left us all—even Preston."

With my father on speaker so Preston could hear what he said, I didn't know what to say. But Preston managed to come up with something. "Her leaving devastated me too, Sloan. And I had no one to share my grief with like you and your father did. Audrey's sudden disappearance worried me to no end. And when the cops came to me, after your father reported her missing, my head was on the chopping block for quite a while. I had to deal with that alone. Richard understood the hardships I'd been through and when we ran into each other again, there were no hard feelings. He and I moved past it all. I don't see why you and I can't."

The idea of my husband and my missing mother having had an affair did something to my gut that nothing ever had. And the knot in my stomach felt as if it might never go away. "I need to be alone." Withdrawing to our bedroom, I found Preston coming in to talk and knew I couldn't let him do that. So, I moved my things to another bedroom, and we stopped sharing a bed. I couldn't let him touch me. Not while knowing that those same hands had been all over my mother.

Each time I looked in the mirror after that, I saw remnants of my mother. Her long dark hair, plump cheeks, rosebud lips, and her big brown eyes looked back at me each time I saw my reflection. It made me sick to think that Preston had once loved her and now he claimed to love me. But maybe he only loved me because of who I reminded him of.

She'd left. At first my father and I had thought the absolute worse. But as time went on and the police did a thorough investigation, it became clear that she'd just left us. Even though Dad hadn't told me about her affair, he had told me that Mom hadn't been happy for quite some time and she must've decided to move on with her life in a direction that didn't include us. With no sign of foul play, both of us thought she'd simply taken off with another man.

The distance between Preston and I grew and grew until one day I came home to find divorce papers. On the table too had been a short note from Preston telling me to leave the car he'd bought for me and to put the keys to the house and the car into the mailbox before I left. He'd put my things in boxes in the backyard and had made temporary arrangements for me to stay a week in a hotel in downtown Austin. Things just weren't going to work out for us. He was deeply sorry and couldn't bear to face me.

Just as I began melting into a puddle of hopelessness, my cell phone rang. Hoping it was Preston telling me he'd reconsidered, I found it was an Uber driver letting me know that she was on her way to pick me up.

Somehow, after all that, I managed to get on my feet without my father's financial help. He was still in Greece and I told him that I wanted to handle things on my own. I had the internship, which didn't pay much, but it was enough for me to get a tiny efficiency apartment on the outskirts of Austin. Plus, a bus pass to get back and forth to work.

When Preston and I had to meet to sign the divorce papers at his attorney's office, guilt got the best of him and he gave the car back to me. I'd always loved the Lincoln MKZ he'd given me as a birthday gift the year before. To have it back made me feel a lot better.

Not long after that, my boss told me that a new resort was about to go up in downtown Austin. He'd gotten a call from the owners about hiring someone new to the construction world. The place was being built by brothers from Houston and they specifically wanted to hire people who needed a chance to get their foot in the door with their new careers. So, with my boss's recommendation, I got the contract to be the structural engineer for Whispers Resort and Spa.

I hoped like hell that starting this new job would bring great changes to my life. I'd worked hard to get my degree and was willing to work hard to prove I could do the job. I didn't want my feminine assets winning me any points, so I had on khaki slacks, a white button-down shirt tucked in, a tan belt, and tan loafers. My dark hair was cut into a short bob and I wore no makeup at all. I wanted to be treated like any other engineer.

With another deep breath, I got out of the car, my laptop bag in hand, and headed to meet the man I'd be working under. Baldwyn Nash would be the man in charge of things—my boss until the project was finished.

The worksite was nothing more than an empty lot with one trailer on it that housed the offices of the people who would build this great facility.

Stepping through the door, I smelled coffee but saw no one in what looked like a tiny, makeshift reception area in what would've been the living room. "Anyone here?"

"Yeah," came a man's deep voice, which got closer as he went on, "the receptionist is late."

My eyes went wide as he stepped around a partition. "Uh, hello."

Tall, dark, and extremely handsome, the man had a muscular build that his expensive black suit clung to as if it had been made to show off that exquisite body. Green eyes shone brightly at me as a smile curved his lips. A strong jaw, square and covered in a dark, neatly trimmed beard made him appear powerful. The dark curls on top of his head were unruly. "Baldwyn Nash." He extended his hand.

I took it, shaking it as I prayed silently that my palm wasn't sweaty. It wasn't easy to pretend his appearance hadn't affected me in a sexual way. He was the hottest man I'd ever had the pleasure of meeting. "Sloan Rivers, your structural engineer. Here and ready to serve you in any way you need." I clamped my mouth shut tightly. *You are in idiot!*

As our hands slipped apart, his smile made me shiver, a thing I hoped he wouldn't notice. "The air conditioning was left on last night. It's like sixty degrees in here. Come on, I'll turn it up some."

Well, crap! He did notice.

"Yeah, it is cold in here." I followed him, my eyes glued to his ass. Ogling men wasn't a thing I often did. But when a man has a butt that just wouldn't quit, I couldn't help but notice. "Is this where my office is going to be?"

"For now, yeah." He turned up the temperature on the thermostat then turned to look at me. "You and I are going to have to share an office for now. But not for too long. More trailers are scheduled to be delivered next week. You'll have one of them at your disposal as lead engineer. That way you can give offices to the people who will work directly under you."

The idea of sharing an office with him, even for a short time, made me happy in a way I couldn't describe. "Good deal, Mr. Nash."

"Baldwyn," he said with a grin. "And may I call you Sloan?"

"Oh yeah, sure, of course you can." My brain wasn't firing on all cylinders with him so close to me in the narrow hallway. He smelled like a forest full of evergreens mixed with the ocean. It was intoxicating. "So, where's this office?"

"I'll show you to it. It's at the other end of the trailer."

"Okay then." My throat went dry and I hated that I'd come to work without bringing so much as a bottle of water.

"I took the room all the way at the end of this hall. It's the largest one. I figured since we have to share, I'd grab this one for us, so we don't get in each other's way."

You'll never be in my way, handsome.

Shaking my head to clear it, I couldn't understand why I was thinking that way. It wasn't like me to react like this. "Good thinking. We don't want to fall all over each other."

His deep chuckle made my heart skip a beat. "Yeah, we don't want that to happen."

Following him into the large room, I saw two empty desks at opposite ends of it. "Have you picked a desk yet?"

"Nope. You can pick first. It doesn't matter to me at all."

Leaning back against the doorframe, he stayed back as I moved into the room, our arms grazing as I moved past him.

Another shiver ran through me with the simple touch. "Still a bit cold in here." I placed my laptop bag on the desk to the right. "Okay, I'll take this one."

"We'd like to make fast progress on this. Will it be a problem for you to work late hours?" He grabbed the chair from the other desk and took a seat, crossing his long legs.

"No, it's not going to be a problem at all. I live alone." The laptop slid out of the bag onto the desk and I smiled for no reason at all. "My divorce became final last month."

"Oh, I'm sorry to hear that."

I looked over my shoulder as the desks faced opposite walls, to find him looking a little sheepish. "Don't be sorry. I'm glad it's over."

"It seems like you're doing well on your own, Sloan." Nodding, his lips pulled up on one side in a half-smile. "But if you need a shoulder to cry on, I've got a couple of broad ones for you. And don't take it the wrong way. As a friend, you know what I mean? You've got a friend in me."

"Thank you." I'd never felt so lucky to have a new friend in my life. "Just getting my career going is such a boost. I'm hoping to buy my own home soon. My tiny efficiency apartment is feeling sort of crowded."

He nodded his head in understanding. "My brothers and I aren't from Austin. We've left our homes in Houston to come build our dream here. We've rented high-end apartments about ten minutes from here. If you'd like, I could get you one too. You can call it a perk. It would be nice to have you close by. You know, so we can work even more hours. But from the comfort of home. It's my understanding that traffic can be a bitch here as well. Having you closer just makes sense."

"I don't know." I was shocked but thrilled by the offer. I

wasn't used to getting the star treatment, so figuring out what to say wasn't easy for me.

"They're completely furnished. All you'd have to do is pack up your clothes and personal items and bring them over. Two bedrooms too. That way you can invite friends and family over." He seemed to be trying to entice me into taking his very generous offer—as if I needed to be convinced.

"I don't have any family here." I didn't want to get into the whole story, so kept it short. "Mom's out of the picture and Dad lives in Greece."

"That's rough." His green eyes never left mine and I saw compassion fill them. "I won't take no for an answer. It's about time you began a new chapter in your life."

Wow, someone who wants to help me start all over again. This is some good luck for once. I wonder how long it'll last ...

3

BALDWYN

IT WAS OBVIOUS THAT SLOAN WASN'T TRYING TO LOOK CUTE ON HER first day of work —tan slacks, white shirt, and loafers, for God's sake. "I've gotta get out of here for a bit, Baldwyn. Missing breakfast isn't a thing I normally do. So, lunch is calling my name a bit early today." Sloan was cute without even trying. I doubted she knew that, but I had noticed it right off the bat.

"Nerves get the best of you this morning?" I knew they had. She'd arrived looking like she was wound as tight as a clock. But now she looked calm, collected, and adorable. And she smiled a lot—something I liked to see.

"I think that's fairly normal for someone who's starting their first job in a new career." Looking around our office, she seemed distracted. "My purse—I can't seem to—" Light laughter filled the room. "Oh, yes, now I remember." Taking the keys from the pocket of her slacks, she headed toward the door. "I left it in my trunk."

Moving in behind her, I caught a whiff of cucumbers as her hair swung back and forth with each step she took. "You were afraid of looking too feminine." It wasn't a question, more like a statement.

The receptionist came in, meeting us in the lobby. "Oh, Mr. Nash. Sorry I'm late. My baby was sick last night and I overslept. I would've called but I was rushing to get dressed and call the sitter to come over."

"You didn't miss anything, Lisa." I didn't want her to think I would always be so lenient though. "But let's not let that happen again. We're not busy at the moment, but soon—like tomorrow—we'll be very busy, and you'll need to be here to answer phone calls and direct people where to go. I expect you to be here at nine—no later than that." It was only her third day on the job. Showing up two hours late didn't bode well for her.

"You've got a baby?" Sloan asked. "A boy or a girl?"

"A girl." Lisa ducked her head as she took the seat behind the desk. "I swear it won't happen again, Mr. Nash."

Sloan looked at me over her shoulder. "I can answer phones if she has problems with her baby, Baldwyn. I don't mind at all." Looking back at Lisa she asked, "Is she your only child, Lisa? Oh, and my name's Sloan Rivers."

Lisa accepted Sloan's extended hand, shaking it as the two smiled at one another. "She is my only child, yes. It's nice to meet you. But aren't you one of the engineers? You can't be answering phones. I'll do what I have to so I won't be late again. Maybe my sister can come over when I'm having trouble with the baby."

"Great idea." I liked a person who could figure things out before they got to be too much of a problem. "We're heading out to lunch. I'll bring something back for you. If you skip your hour lunch break and both thirty-minute breaks, I won't have to dock your pay for your tardiness."

"Thanks, boss." Lisa pulled open the drawer of her desk to get to work. "I really appreciate you doing that for me. Anything you bring back for me will be fine, sir."

"So, we get an hour lunch?" Sloan asked as we headed outside.

The noise of traffic moving by on the interstate ablock over made it hard to hear, so I had to speak a bit louder than I had been. "We get as long as we want." I stepped in beside her, steering her toward my car. "You like sushi?"

Stopping, she looked me square in the eye. "You don't have to come to lunch with me."

"You're coming with *me*." Bumping her shoulder with mine, I moved her farther in the direction I wanted her to go in. "Come on, I'll drive. Lunch is on me. It's a write-off, so don't argue about it."

"And the apartment?" she asked as the argument I'd half-expected from her didn't come.

"Yes, it'll be a write-off too. So, I don't want you thinking I'm doing you any real favors. I've got my financial reasons for giving you all I'm going to give you. How's your car situation? Do you have a reliable one?"

"I do have a reliable car. No need to get me one." Running her hand through her hair, she smiled as she looked up at the bright blue sky. "It's nice out today." She looked at my car as I hit the key fob to unlock it, then her eyes met mine. "What do you say to eating al fresco, instead of sushi?"

"Do you know a place?" I didn't know much about the surrounding area yet.

"Joe's makes insane street tacos. You into Tex-Mex?"

"I'm from Houston, Sloan. Tex-Mex is life there." I held the car door open for her and she looked up at me, as I was a good foot taller than her. "So, Joe's it is."

"Thanks, Baldwyn." Taking a seat, she put on her seatbelt as I closed the door.

The traffic was stop and go and I knew I should've been used to it since I was from a big city as well, but this was worse. I didn't understand why. "This traffic is out of this world."

"Yeah," she agreed. "The population has been booming in recent years. Seems the city is having a hard time keeping up. It'll be great to have a restaurant inside the resort so people don't have to leave to get something to eat."

The GPS told me that Joe's was just ahead on the right. A line of people went around the corner and my mouth began to water. "Looks like this is a great place to eat."

"It is," she gushed. "One of the best. They close at three each day, so people have to get his tacos while they can."

It took an act of congress to find a parking spot, but once I did, we both nearly sprinted to get a place in the long line. My cell rang just as we got in line. "My brother, Stone," I let her know as I swiped the screen. "What's up, baby brother?"

"I'm at the stop light right behind you. What are you doing and who are you with?" he asked.

Turning to find him, I saw his car and three more heads were in it. "You brought the pack, huh?"

"Yeah, we all rode in together. Do I smell tacos?"

"You do. You should park and come join us. Our lead engineer, Sloan Rivers, says they're great."

"So that's who she is," he said with a laugh. "Get a table big enough for all of us."

Ending the call, I grinned at Sloan. "You're going to get to meet my brothers."

Tension made her body ridged as her jaw clenched. "Oh, good."

"You're not nervous, are you?" I asked.

"What's to be nervous about?" Her hands fisted at her sides. "It's just lunch with five men who happen to be my bosses."

I didn't want her to think of us in that regard at all. "Sloan, you're not working under any of us. You're a contractor, not an employee."

"Yeah." A slight nod made me think she was trying to get used to the idea. I knew this was her first solo project, so I figured it might take some adjusting. "It's just that I've always worked for someone—never for myself. But you're right. You gentlemen are more like my clients than my bosses."

"We *are* your clients." Inhaling the delicious scent of cilantro, I moaned a bit. "I can't wait to taste these tacos."

"It won't be much longer." Nodding to the fast-moving line she said, "Only five more, then our turn."

"Having a local as a friend seems to be paying off for me already." I saw my brothers coming our way. "Here comes the rat-pack now."

Their hurry to get places in the long line made their greetings short as they all said in unison, "Nice to meet you, Sloan."

She waved and shouted as they ran to the back of the line, "Nice meeting y'all too."

Fifteen minutes later, Sloan and I sat at an umbrella-covered table, a cool breeze blowing her dark hair around her makeup-free face. Her doe-like didn't need a bunch of mascara and eyeliner to make them look pretty. Thick, dark lashes made them pop on their own. A light pink blush stained the apples of her cheeks, matching the shade of her plump lips.

It was hard to tell exactly what sort of figure she had with the shapeless slacks and button-down shirt she wore. But I wasn't supposed to be checking her out in that way anyway. So, I diverted my attention by watching her expertly splash something red onto her taco. "Is that spicy?"

"It sure is." She pushed the bottle to me. "You've got to try some."

"Do I have to?" Opening the lid, I took a sniff. "It smells pretty hot."

"Only because it is." She took a big bite, nodding as she chewed and made a satisfied moan. "So good."

I carefully splashed one drop onto the top of my beef fajita taco. I wasn't about to drench it the way she had. "Let me see about this stuff before I slather it on."

"It's garlic and chilies combined with vinegar and what tastes a lot like coconut oil to me. Tell me what you think it is." Her eyes stayed glued to mine as I took my first bite.

Heat filled my mouth. "Chilies!" Lots and lots of spicy chili peppers were evident in the sauce. But then the heat faded enough that I could taste the garlic and the slightest hint of coconut. "You're right, there's some coconut oil in this. It's good!" I poured more on then took another bite.

"I can't wait to taste these," Stone said as he took the empty seat next to Sloan. "I'm Stone, Sloan."

"Nice to meet you." She held up her taco that took two hands to hold. "I'd shake your hand, but as you can see, mine are full."

"As mine soon will be." Stone looked at the sauce I had near me. "Is that any good?"

"No," I said with a grin. "It's great!" I pushed it to him as Patton came to sit next to me. "This is Patton. Patton, Sloan."

"It's great to meet you, Sloan. I can't wait to work with you." He scooted his chair over a bit as Cohen came to sit next to him. "Sloan, this is Cohen."

Cohen nodded. "It's nice to meet you."

"Same. Try the sauce." She moved it his way. "It's really good."

Warner came in last, taking the place next to Stone. "Hey, Sloan, I'm Warner. How's Baldwyn been treatin' ya so far?"

"Great." She looked right at me and her dark eyes shined. "He's treating me to lunch and has already offered me a new place to live."

"Cool, you're going to move into the complex with us?" Warner asked as he poured the sauce over his taco.

She hadn't given me a real answer. I'd told her that I wasn't going to take no for an answer, but that didn't mean she had agreed. So, I waited and watched her expression morph from a smile to a frown, then back to a smile again before she said, "Yeah. I am going to move into the complex. I think it'll be quite an experience for me."

"That's good, Sloan." I couldn't wipe the smile off my face. "It is going to be quite the experience for all of us. Glad to have you onboard."

Her eyes sweeping around the table, she took each of us in before she said, "Your mother and father must be proud to have such a handsome bunch of sons."

"I'm sure they were," I said then picked up a napkin to wipe my face. "They died in a housefire."

Her jaw dropped as her eyes went wide. Stone nudged her shoulder with his. "It's okay, Sloan. It was like sixteen years ago. I was eight when they died. But Baldwyn was nineteen. He took good care of us."

Patton added, "I helped too, even though I was just sixteen and still in school."

"I was thirteen and Cohen was eleven," Warner said. "Our older brothers had their work cut out for them, wrangling us three. But they did it somehow."

"And you all have achieved so much already," she whispered as if she couldn't believe it.

"Yeah, we worked through it." I'd never thought of us as unfortunate. I'd always felt like our parent's deaths had served to make us all a lot stronger. "They were alone at the house that morning, since my brothers were at school and I'd gone to my job as a busboy at a resort near our house. I heard the sirens from there. It never occurred to me that they were going to our house."

"The school nurse came to get me out of class," Stone said as he looked off in the distance. "She told me that they'd lost their lives in a fire and I really didn't know what that meant at all. I kept asking where Mom and Dad were. I knew they lost their lives but had no idea that meant their bodies too."

Warner smiled. "Little goof."

"I was," Stone admitted.

Sloan put her hand on his shoulder as her brow furrowed. "No, you weren't a goof. You were a child who didn't understand things like death yet. That must've been horrible for you guys."

I barely remembered that time. "It was a blur. We had no home as the fire had completely destroyed it. We only had the clothes on our backs. I'd taken my car to work, so we had that. An old Chevy Nova with no air conditioning. Mom's and Dad's cars were in the garage and they burned as well."

"It's a miracle that you all have done so well." Holding her hand over her heart, she cocked her head as she looked at me. "What a great father you must have become to your brothers, Baldwyn." Respect filled her dark eyes. "What a great man you are," she said so quietly I almost missed it.

"I just did what had to be done, is all." I never liked to take credit for being anything other than a responsible human being who knew he had to take care of the only family he had left.

The adoration that radiated off her sure did make me feel super-human though. *I bet I could fly right now if I really tried.*

4

SLOAN

Heading back to the office, I had a whole new respect for Baldwyn Nash. "So, taking on the role of father at only nineteen. Wow."

The way his broad shoulders moved a bit told me he didn't think it was that big of a deal. "You never know what you can do until you're put in the position to do it. If anyone would've asked me if I could've finished raising my four brothers, I would've told them there would be no way in hell. But when you're faced with doing something or handing it over to someone else, something as important as your siblings, then you find yourself doing whatever it takes to make it work.."

"You lost your home too." I couldn't imagine losing so much at one time. "What did you guys end up doing?"

"My boss let us stay in the penthouse suite for nearly a year. I didn't want to be beholden to him, though. I wanted to be able to change employment. So, I took a loan from our Uncle Rob and moved my brothers and I into a three-bedroom apartment." He said it like it was no big deal.

"I think you're more of a hero than you think you are. Even when it comes to giving people a shot that most wouldn't. Like me, for instance." I felt extremely lucky that he'd seen fit to give me the shot that I hoped would set off my career.

Pulling into the worksite, he just smiled. "You deserve the chance to start your business, Sloan. You made excellent grades in college and had stellar reviews from your internship. They made it clear they would snatch you up themselves if I didn't hire you. You've earned this chance."

"I have tried." Warmth spread over my cheeks, as I wasn't used to being complimented. "I will do everything I can to make you proud that you hired me to build your resort."

"I'm sure you will." Taking the bag with the tacos he'd brought for Lisa, he got out of the car and so did I.

I followed behind him, ducking my head as I didn't want anyone to see the huge smile I wore. Just being in the man's company made me feel awesome. Although I was deeply attracted to him physically, I wasn't about to do anything about that. I wanted us to have a professional relationship. I knew people could be friends who worked together—but becoming lovers most often led to bad situations. Plus, I respected the hell out of the man.

Thinking about Baldwyn in a romantic way wasn't what I was supposed to be doing. And being that it was my first day at work, that *really* wasn't supposed to be happening.

"I smell Joe's tacos," Lisa greeted us as we came into the tiny reception area. Her golden eyes met mine. "I can thank you for this, I'm sure, Sloan."

"I did introduce him to one of Austin's best kept secrets. His brothers were introduced to Joe's as well. All loved the tacos and the insane sauce."

She took the brown bag from Baldwyn. "Oh, please tell me that you snagged me a bit of that amazing sauce."

"I did better than snagging you a bit, Lisa." Baldwyn grinned, proud of his magnificent feat. "Look in the bag."

With wide eyes, Lisa opened the bag and pulled out a long glass bottle filled with the red sauce that Baldwyn had paid through the nose for after a lengthy battle with Joe. "No way!"

"Yup." Baldwyn polished his nails on his lapel. "Joe doesn't sell his sauce, so getting him to give me the bottle wasn't easy."

Clutching the glass container to her chest, her eyes shined as she looked adoringly at him. "How did you accomplish this, boss?"

Putting his finger to his lips, he said, "Hush-hush. We don't want everyone thinking we'll give away nights at our resort for one bottle of anything."

Cutting her eyes at me, she asked, "How many bottles did he get?"

"Only the one." I was a little jealous of her—in more ways than one. But I was more in awe of Baldwyn for the reason he bought it for her in the first place. "Your boss is very empathetic, it seems. He thought about your hard night with your baby girl and decided to get you something nice."

"No," she whispered. "Just for that?"

With that careless shrug of his massive shoulders I'd seen a few times now, Baldwyn wasn't going to let her, or me, make a big deal out of it. "Hey, it's just some hot sauce. No biggie."

"It *is* a biggie and I love it, boss. I truly do." Lisa looked as if she was about to get up.

But he stopped her. "Don't get mushy on me, Lisa. No hugs necessary." Turning to face me, he eyed me for a moment. "What's your favorite color, Sloan?"

"Burnt orange."

I was a Texan through and through. But he wasn't interested in my college colors. "I mean, what colors do you like in a home? The walls, carpets, flooring in general? And the curtains, bedspreads, those sorts of things?"

"Oh." I looked at Lisa, who'd begun to ignore us as she took out her tacos. "Come, let's talk about this in our office, shall we?" I saw no need to make her jealous about what Baldwyn was giving me.

Taking a seat in my chair, I watched him roll his own chair about a foot away from mine.

"So, the colors?"

"Anything is fine, Baldwyn. Just the fact that you're putting me up is a privilege."

"So, there's neutral colors, evening colors, morning colors, and afternoon colors." Handing me his cell phone, I saw he'd already pulled up the apartment complex's website. "Pick one."

I didn't need to see pictures to know what I wanted. "I'm a morning person, so I'll take that one." Handing him the phone, a short electric shock went up my arm as our fingers barely touched. I'd never felt anything like that in my life.

"I'm into mornings too." Pursing his lips for only a moment, he sighed. "You'll like the color scheme. Pinks, blues, oranges, yellows, all pastel, of course. The master bedroom has this huge window that gives you a view of the eastern sky. The sunrises so far have been off the charts."

Sunrises had always been one of my favorite things in the world. "Oh, yeah?" Preston didn't share my love for the early morning. He always preferred late nights. But Baldwyn and I were sort of syncing.

Putting the phone on speaker, he made the call to the apartment complex.

"Vista Estates," a woman answered.

"Pam?" he asked.

"Yes, this is she."

"It's Baldwyn Nash."

"Oh, yes. What can I do for you, sir?" Her eager response told me he'd already spent lots of money there.

"Do you happen to have a morning-scheme apartment available?" he asked, grinning at me as if he knew something I didn't.

I heard tapping as she must've been looking at her computer. "I have three, sir. One's right next to yours."

"I'll take that one," he said quickly. Putting the phone on mute, he told me, "My place is right by the pool. That means yours will be too. Another pleasant perk."

"Of course," Pam answered. "When will you want that, sir?"

"When can we have it?" Drumming his fingers on his thick leg, his eyes were glued to mine.

"It's ready now," she said. "I can email you the lease for you to e-sign and I already have your billing information on file. This will be a Whispers Resort business lease, right?"

"It will. Send me the lease and I'll have it back to you soon." His grin made me shiver with delight.

"I'll open the apartment myself and leave the key code and a copy of the signed lease on the counter in the kitchen. I only need the name of the people who will reside there, a copy of their driver's licenses, and the plate numbers and makes and models of any cars that they'll park there."

"Sloan Rivers." He gave me a wink. "A black Lincoln MKZ, plate number RIV002. And she'll text you a copy of her license."

"Great. I'll get that lease sent to you very soon, Mr. Baldwyn. Goodbye."

He'd astonished me. "You memorized that?" I hadn't noticed him giving my car any attention at all.

"Yeah." Putting his cell into his breast pocket, he asked, "So, the plate—what's that mean?"

I wasn't happy with the license plate of my car. But I couldn't change it anytime soon. "My ex registers his plates that way. RIV is for Rivers and then he gives the cars numbers. Mine was 002 and his was 001. Stupid, I know."

"And you're sure you wouldn't like me to get you another

car?" He rolled his chair to his desk. "Because if it bothers you to have things he gave you, it's not a problem in the least to get you a car. I can have one here before the end of the day."

It was nice to know that he had my back if I really needed that sort of thing. "I like my car. But if it gets to be a problem, then I'll definitely take you up on the offer. And thank you for the apartment." I had no idea what sort of problems I would have getting out of my current lease. But I wasn't about to say a thing about that to him.

"You bring in the bill your current apartment sends you for breaking the lease and we'll take care of it." He opened the desk and pulled out a laptop computer.

Is he psychic? "Are you sure about that?" I didn't want to be a bother. "I should get on the phone with the cable company to get my services transferred."

"Nah, the complex is all-inclusive. No need to transfer anything—electric, internet, cable—they're already on. Just turn off the services you currently have."

"So, I won't have any bills at all?" I felt as if this was too good to be true. "Baldwyn, I can't." I felt that wasn't a strong enough word. "No, I *won't* be a kept woman."

Slowly, he turned to me, his green eyes set on mine. "This is a *business* dealing, Sloan. You're not kept in any way. I won't have access to your home. No one will. You're not expected to do anything for me or my brothers or anyone connected with this endeavor except legit business. Tell me you understand that clearly."

"Now I do." For a moment I felt stupid for what I'd said. "Sorry. My marriage has kind of messed me up. Thank you for this business opportunity and the perks that go with it. I appreciate it and I promise to try extremely hard to believe in the best here."

"You should believe in it. I'm your client and I am your

friend. Nothing more than that, Sloan. Nothing." Getting up, he walked out of the office.

I put my face in my hands. He came back in with two bottles of water and nudged me with one. "Oh, you're back."

"Yeah. So, let's get to work, shall we? I can't wait to see what you've come up with so far. This is my dream and I'm hoping we can make it the way I want to. And if we can't, then I hope you can come up with something I'll at least like."

"Like?" I wasn't about to let him settle with just liking something. I wanted him to love it. All of it. "Oh, I'll make sure we can get this resort the way you want it. I want a five-star review from you, Baldwyn Nash. When this is all said and done, I want you and your brothers to love what we've built."

"I'm sure we will love it, Sloan." He eased back in his chair, hands behind his head, closing his eyes as if seeing the sight of the finished resort in his mind.

And all I could do was gaze at him with adoration. *I hope he's not too good to be true.*

5

BALDWYN

A MONTH INTO THE PROJECT, THINGS WERE GOING SMOOTHLY. I had to hand it to Sloan, who had no problem managing the other engineers, for keeping things moving forward.

Meeting the Gentrys' private plane at the airport, I picked up Tyrell who had flown into Austin to make a quick visit to the worksite.

Sliding into the front passenger seat, he smiled at me. "You're looking happy, Baldwyn. Things must be going great."

"They are." Taking off to get him downtown, I couldn't wipe the smile off my face. "We've made some great connections with the contractors we've hired. I think our idea of hiring newbies was a good idea."

"I wasn't so sure about that," he admitted. "But I didn't want to stomp on your dreams either. I'm glad it's working out for you."

I noticed that he hadn't brought an overnight bag. "You're leaving today?"

"Yeah. I'm just going to check things out then get back on the plane and get back home. I don't like sleeping without my girl.

And the ride back home is less than an hour, so why stay overnight?"

"I get it." It had been a while since my last relationship. Work took up all my time now, so sex wasn't at the forefront of my mind. But it was there, lingering in the back, especially anytime Sloan was around. Not that I'd acted on the attraction.

"How ya likin' these Austin chicks?" Looking out the window, he craned his neck to see the tall buildings as we drove down the interstate into the heart of downtown.

"I've been a bit too busy to worry about anything like that." Taking the exit, I pointed out the empty space in the skyline that one day would be filled with our resort. "There's the spot right there. They tore down a crumbling parking garage a year and a half ago. If it weren't for, there wouldn't be a spot for another building down here."

"That was some good luck." He got out of the truck after I parked. Looking at the work going on and the progress so far, he seemed impressed. "You got things happening here, Baldwyn. Are you on schedule?"

"We *are* on schedule. Our lead engineer makes sure of it each and every day." Leading him into the trailer that housed the engineers' offices, I found Sloan and Rey, the industrial engineer we'd hired, about to walk out the door. "Oh, hey, you guys taking off?"

"We were going for coffee," Sloan said as she backed up, taking Rey by the shoulder and pulling him with her. "But since you're here, we'll do that later." Her eyes went to Tyrell, who came in behind me. "This has got to be Tyrell Gentry." She reached around me to shake his hand. "Your cousin has told me so much about you."

Shaking her hand, he gave her a broad smile. "All good things, I hope."

"Of course." She let his hand go and gestured to the man

standing beside her. "This is Rey Delaney. He's an engineer on this project."

Tyrell shook his hand too. "It's a pleasure, Rey."

"For me too." Rey moved back to take a seat at the long table where we had our meetings each morning.

"My cousin is here to check things out," I let them know. "Sloan, care to fill him in on the progress?"

"Sure thing." She took the seat next to mine as Tyrell sat across the table from us. Pulling the stack of the day's papers toward her, she leafed through them then pulled one out and slid it to him. "This is the timeline. As you can see by the green line, we're on schedule."

I leaned back in my chair, happy with her confidence. "Sloan's my right hand."

"And sometimes I'm your left hand too," she said with a grin. "I try to get things done before Baldwyn even asks for it."

"Sounds good," Tyrell said with a nod. "It looks like you've built a great team here, Baldwyn."

Sloan stood. "If you need me for anything else, just shoot me a text. I've got to get out on the ground to make sure the crews keep it going. If I don't check up on them at least once an hour, I find them slacking off. And we cannot have any slacking."

"Engineer *and* crew chief?" Tyrell asked her.

"I'm whatever I have to be to keep things running smoothly." Patting me on the back, she leaned in. "If I need to find another ride home, I can."

"Nah, I'll be back in time to take you home." I liked sharing the short rides to and from the apartment complex with her.

"Okay then." She and Rey left us alone.

I hadn't realized that I'd been watching her departing form until the door closed. I turned to see Tyrell grinning at me. "Oh, hell, man. You like her."

"Sure I do."

"No." He shook his head. "I mean that you *like* her." Seeing my tight-lipped face, he continued, "In a romantic way."

"Nah." I did but I wasn't going to act on it.

"Maybe after the business is done, then you'll make your move." Crossing his arms over his chest, he seemed to think he'd figured me out. "Smart, Baldwyn."

"I'm not sure I'll ever make a move on Sloan. She's got something in her recent past that makes that a bad idea." I didn't like talking behind people's backs. But I hadn't been able to say a thing to any of my brothers about Sloan for fear they'd run their mouths.

Steepling his fingers, Tyrell placed his elbows on the table and leaned forward. "And that is?"

"She's only twenty-eight and already divorced. Her entire adult life she's been in a relationship with the same man. She's even told me that her husband—now ex—is the only man she's ever had sex with." Clamping my mouth shut, I knew I wasn't supposed to repeat that to anyone. Not that Sloan had told me not to say anything, but it was pretty obvious that she didn't tell everyone that tidbit of information.

"And what had you guys talking about a thing like that?" he asked with a knowing grin. "Maybe you and she are both thinking about the same thing here. And maybe she's more into it than you think she is."

"She's not." I was sure of that. "She's still dealing with some things from their breakup. She hasn't told me that, but I can tell. Something is unresolved, I think. Not that I think she still loves the guy or anything. Just that she's got something she'd like to finish with him."

"And that makes you nervous," he said. "Like she might get back together with him to resolve this unfinished business."

I hadn't thought about it that way at all. "Well, I don't know. I mean, I've been telling myself that this is business and we can be friends but nothing more than that. And I think we're great friends. We also work great together. Everything is great, is what I'm trying to say."

"Yeah, I got that much." He chuckled, amused with my ramblings.

"Anyway, I'm just saying that neither of us has made a move and that tells me she's not ready for romance of any kind."

"She ran her hand along your back, Baldwyn. She's ready."

"It was a pat." *Was it more than just a pat?*

"No, it wasn't a pat. She ran her hand all the way along the top of your back. And you know what that means?" The gleam in his eye told me that he thought it meant something other than what I had in mind..

"Well, even if she did that—which I don't think she really did as much as you think you saw—it doesn't matter." I'd made up my mind. "We're working together, so sex is out."

"What about romance?" he asked as he got up. "Romance and sex are not one and the same. You could woo her slowly."

"Woo her?" I couldn't help but laugh at his archaic language.

"What if her ex comes back into her life?"

I didn't think that would happen. But if it did, I didn't think I would like it much at all. "He's never supported her career choice. I don't think he'll be into her with her having this job now."

"Yeah, you might be right. Or you might be wrong. Seeing that she's capable of doing this job just might bring his light back on for her. Whose light went out anyway?"

I had no idea. "Not sure. Don't care. It's not my business. But whatever happens, happens. I know from the past that I can't manipulate anyone's life. And I don't want to."

"I see." Tyrell didn't see at all though. "You're willing to let that guy take her back before you declare your feelings for her?"

"I am not." I wasn't going to let her ex take her back. "I mean

—hell, I don't know what I mean. He wasn't good for her. He tried like hell to hold her back. But she kept on moving forward anyway. I respect that in a person. I really respect that in a woman who was married to the person who was trying to keep her from reaching her goal."

"I've found out that respect is just another word for love." He said as if it were true.

"You're crazy. Respect is respect and that's it. I respect her and I know she respects me." That was enough for me. "Her friendship is more than enough for me."

Looking out the door, he leaned on the frame, inhaling the dust stirred up by the digging machines. "I just hope her ex doesn't show up and fuck up all this great work."

"She wouldn't let him." I felt almost certain of that.

6

SLOAN

Closing the refrigerator door after finding little in it, I knew it was time to make a grocery run, even though it was the last thing I felt like doing on a Sunday morning. "If I want to eat, I have to shop."

Grabbing my purse on the way out, I stopped on the front porch, looking at Baldwyn's door. *Maybe I should see if he'd like me to pick up anything.*

Giving my cell a glance, I saw it was only seven in the morning. That seemed a bit too early to be knocking on anyone's door—even if he was up already. Sunday was the only day we all took off work. I couldn't risk waking him up.

As I pulled into the nearly empty parking lot of my favorite grocery store, I felt happy that I wouldn't have to fight a crowd. Taking my time meant I'd find better bargains than if I had to rush.

The produce smelled fresh as I entered the store. That was one of the main reasons I loved this particular grocery store so much—the fresh fruits and veggies. As I picked up a pear, taking a sniff of it, I thought about making something nice for lunch. I could invite Baldwyn and his brothers over to enjoy the meal too.

Sunday lunches sounded like a great thing to start doing with my new friends. So, I took out my cell to look up recipes for something special to make. Scrolling through the many ideas that popped up, I found what I wanted to serve for our first ever Sunday lunch. "Roasted chicken with asparagus and portabella mushrooms." Licking my lips, I went to pick out some fresh greens to make a salad to go with it.

"You're up early." The man's voice made chills run down my spine.

My shoulders tensed as I eased my head to the side to find my ex-husband coming toward me. "So are you." He'd never gotten up before ten o'clock before. "This is odd."

"Why?" He pushed his cart up next to mine then let go of it to open his arms.

I looked at them then shook my head. "No hugs, Preston."

"I see." Shoving his hands into the pockets of his slacks, he frowned at me. "It's not like we parted on terrible terms, you know. I don't know why we can't be cordial to one another."

"Am I screaming and running away from you?" I didn't know what he expected from me. "And we didn't exactly part on the best of terms either. It's been months since I've even seen you."

"Two months. Not since the divorce hearing. I have to admit I have missed seeing your face."

Blood began to boil in my veins—my face and my mother's face were very much the same. "Only that, huh? Wonder why that is."

"We've been together for ten years, Sloan. I've grown accustomed to seeing that face of yours." Reaching out, he tried to run his fingers over my cheek, the way he'd done millions of times before.

Moving back, my eyes narrowed. "No touching, Preston."

"You are in a mood, aren't you?" Shoving his hands back into his pockets, he seemed to have to house them or he'd keep trying to touch me. "How's life treating you?"

"Great, actually. I've got a job now. One that will surely spark my career as an engineer." It satisfied me to no end to see the glisten in his pale blue eyes.

"Good for you, proving me wrong." A half-cocked smile told me I'd surprised him. "And where are you residing now? I've gone by your place and the car I gave you hasn't been there in a month."

"I've moved into an apartment near the worksite. Quite a few of us moved in there while the construction phase is going on. It makes it easier to keep things on track." I didn't want to say too much about how I got the apartment, afraid he'd make a big deal about it.

"The pay must be good if you were able to move." Shuffling a bit, he looked up at the ceiling. "But of course it has to be good if you've been hired as an engineer."

"Yes, the pay is good." I didn't want to chit chat with my ex. "I've got to get my grocery shopping done."

Before he could say anything else, my cell rang and I pulled it out of my pocket, finding it was Baldwyn. Swiping the screen, I didn't get to say a word as he said, "Where'd ya go?"

"To the store. You need anything while I'm here?" I tried to ignore Preston's disturbed expression. He wasn't used to me having friends, since he'd monopolized my time since I was eighteen.

"No. But I did want to ask you about lunch today. Wanna go somewhere?"

"I was thinking about cooking a meal for you and your brothers. But if you'd rather go out, that works too." It became harder to ignore Preston, who was now watching me with a frown.

"Don't cook. Let's go out. I want you to show me around your town. Wanna leave around eleven?"

"Sure. I'll get finished up here at the store then I'll be home. See ya soon." I ended the call then put my phone back into my pocket. "Well, I need to get going, Preston. It was nice seeing you again. You take care."

Before I could speed off, he caught me by the arm. "Who was that? I heard a man's voice. And you said you were going to make something for him and his brothers. What's that about? Do you two live together?"

"That was the man I work for. We don't live together. He's my next-door neighbor though, and his brothers live in the same complex." It wasn't any of his business and I had no idea why I was even answering his questions. But there I was, answering away.

A perturbed expression told me he wasn't keen on anything I'd said thus far. "You're going out with this guy?"

"Not like a date. We're just friends." Did I want to be more than just friends with Baldwyn? Sure. But things hadn't exactly gone in that direction yet.

"I don't think going out with a man is in your best interests," he stated, as if he had any idea what I wanted or needed in my life.

"I'm not going to just sit home and grow old alone, Preston." I pushed my cart away from him, walking quickly.

"Dating a man you work with isn't a good idea." He had no problem keeping up with me.

"We're not dating. As usual, you're not listening to me." The whole idea of shopping had flown out the window. Now all I wanted to do was get the hell away from my ex.

"You're lying to me, Sloan. That sounded like a date to me."

"I don't know what else I can say to you."

"Say you won't go. Call him back and tell him that you can't go." He grabbed my upper arm to stop me from hauling ass away from him. "Please."

Looking at his hold on me, I gritted my teeth. "Let me go right now."

Easing his hand off me, he looked a little sheepish. "Sloan, I am sorry about that. But you're not ready to date. We were together for a long time. You've always thought you were a lot stronger than you actually are. I don't want to see you get hurt."

Like finding out you fucked my mother for a couple of years didn't hurt me!

"Don't worry about me, Preston." Abandoning my shopping cart, I turned away from him and walked toward the exit.

"As if I can help worrying about you, Sloan. You're my wife!" he called out after me.

Spinning back around, I felt the heat of anger flush my face. "*Was* your wife. I'm not anymore." Then I turned and left the store.

What a fucking jackass. How did I ever love him?

7

BALDWYN

Sloan had no idea how cute she looked in her shorts and tank top.

"So, none of your brothers wanted to come with us?"

"No." I hadn't asked them to come. "I think they had other plans." I just wanted today to be about the two of us. My dreams the night before had gotten on the racy side and Sloan had starred in them all. Sharing her attention just wasn't going to do it for me today.

Sweeping her dark hair up then wrapping it with a rubber band, she put it into a high ponytail that made her look even more adorable. "Well that's too bad because they're going to miss out on this little-known pub that makes Sundays awesome."

With a dark wooden exterior and a huge green door, the pub looked as if it had traveled through a wormhole from ancient Ireland before settling in the outskirts of Austin. "Is this one of those places where the waitresses dress in period clothing?" Boobs bursting out of the tops of tight blouses sounded appealing.

"Not at all." Turning to me as she walked backward toward the door, she smiled knowingly. "Are you disappointed?"

"Not at all." Sloan had some things going on herself that would keep my eyes occupied.

Pushing the heavy door open, she held it for me. "Gentlemen first."

"Okay, then." I walked inside the dark corridor; a green light shone at the end of it. "That way, I assume." Laughter and clinking glass met my ears. "Sounds like the fun's already started."

"It's one on a Sunday afternoon," she said as she walked up beside me. "I'm sure the crowd is pretty much drunk already."

A glowing flatscreen television the size of a dining room table hung above the long bar, littered with men and women. "Soccer fans."

"And Gaelic football too," she said as she took a seat at a small table for two at the back of the room. "These guys get really loud when that stuff comes on."

I had the idea she wanted a liquid lunch. "I can't imagine you brought me here for the food."

"You'll see. They make the best pot roast I've ever tasted. Tiny pearl onions, green peas, and this thick dark gravy that defies imagination. Makes this place one of my favorite food spots in Austin." She held up her hand, signaling a waitress.

"I said *I* was going to take you out. How did you manage to take this lunch over, Sloan Rivers?" I'd wanted to take her someplace nice and quiet, but she had other ideas. She'd even made me ride with her, taking her car. How had I lost control?

The waitress brought two frosty mugs. "What shall I fill these with?"

"Guinness," Sloan told her. "Can we get the house special with lots of soda bread?"

"Got it." The waitress placed the mugs on the table, then took off, heading back to the bar.

"This is quaint." It was loud and dark, not at all what I'd been planning. But when the food and drinks arrived, I dug in after the first bite. "Sloan, yes! Winner!"

"I know." She dunked a chunk of bread into the beefy gravy. "We're going to need a nap after this."

"I call your couch," I said before gulping down the dark beer.

Shrugging her narrow shoulders, she seemed cool with my idea of napping over at her place. "As long as you leave some room for me, we're cool."

Napping together on her couch? Hell yeah!

"Who's your friend, Sloan?" a man asked from out of nowhere. He held a mug of beer in one hand and the other fisted at his side as he stood next to Sloan.

"What the hell?" She looked up at him with wide eyes. "What are you doing here?"

The man was older than her. I figured it must be a friend of her father's or something as he seemed to be in his fifties. He had salt and pepper hair, a strong jawline, and his pale blue eyes stared right at me. "I'm Preston Rivers."

"Oh, shit!" I hadn't meant for that to come out of my mouth. "I mean, hi."

"This is Baldwyn." Sloan's aggravation at her ex was evident in her voice.

"I thought you said this wasn't a date, Sloan." His eyes were still on me. "I'm her husband. Surely she's told you about me."

"She's said a bit. Mostly that you're not her husband anymore." I picked up my mug of beer to take a drink and to stop myself from saying anything totally stupid—like "*get the fuck out of here, you're being a total cock-blocker, you old fuck.*"

"Preston, just leave." Her cheeks were as red as a tomato. Anger bubbled inside of her, making her shake a bit.

I didn't like what I saw. "You should do what she says, man."

Apparently, he didn't like me telling him what to do. His eyes lit up as if I'd smacked him in the face with a white glove, silently demanding a duel. "You should mind your business, boy."

No one had called me boy in years. But Sloan's pleading gaze told me not to take the carrot that her ex dangled in front of me. I could totally kick the old fart's ass if I wanted.

"Preston, please," she whimpered.

I hated hearing her speak that way. She was a strong woman in every other way. This jerk-off made her drift right back into what he'd molded her into—a doormat for him to scrape his dirty feet on. And I wasn't going to let him do that to her.

"She's not as strong as you think she is, Baldwyn," he said, his eyes softening. "Toying with her will only leave her with scars on her psyche."

"Dude, I'm not toying with her. You seem to be though. And I think that's pretty fucking shitty of you, to be honest," I said. "She's one hell of a person. Sorry you didn't see that before."

Squaring her shoulders, Sloan took a deep breath then got up to face the man she'd been married to. "Leave."

"Come with me, baby." He tried to take her hands in his.

With a quick step back, she evaded him. "Don't call me that. Leave. Now."

His shoulders sagged and his lips turned into the shape of a horseshoe. "Fine." He stepped back then looked at me. "Your ass will be mine if you hurt her."

Isn't that ironic? So many things popped into my head to say to the man who'd obviously hurt her. But all I did was nod. I saw no reason to give him an opportunity to stay and talk more shit to me.

Sloan stood there, watching him until he placed his mug on the bar then walked out the door. Only then did she take her seat, staring with glazed eyes at her plate. "I'm sorry about all that."

"And embarrassed." I saw it on her face. "Don't be. You can't control him." I took a drink of the ale then sat it down on the table. "But I've got to be honest with you."

"I know. I was weak." A long sigh came out of her mouth.

She had no idea what I was really thinking. "Not at all. You stood your ground, Sloan. I'm proud of you. Fucking proud." Grabbing my mug, I held it up. "A toast to you, fiery maiden!"

Others around us held up their mugs too as they'd witnessed the whole thing. "Fiery maiden!" they all echoed me.

A smile broke free from her pink lips and she picked up her mug, clanking it against mine. "Thank you."

8

SLOAN

AFTER GETTING HOME FROM THE BAR, I LAID ON ONE END OF MY sofa while Baldwyn laid on the other. Pulling off my shoes, he massaged one foot. "You need to relax, girl."

"I know I do." I'd been more than relaxed before my stupid ex showed up to ruin my Sunday Funday. "The day didn't turn out the way I wanted it to."

"I don't know," Baldwyn said as he smiled at me. "We *are* about to nap on your couch the way we'd planned on doing. He didn't ruin that."

But Preston had ruined lunch. We'd left only a few minutes after he'd interrupted what had been a scrumptious meal. "I bet you're wondering what I ever saw in that man."

"Nah." His fingers moved along the base of my toes, putting exactly enough pressure on them to make me moan a bit. "You like that?"

"Yesssss," I moaned. "You're good at this."

Waggling his dark brows, he made me smile. "One day I'll give you a backrub and show you how good I can really be."

"I should be so lucky." It felt good being with him. Preston had never catered to me in any way. Certainly not the way Baldwyn was now.

Baldwyn's eyelids began to droop as the beer and heavy food began taking him away to dreamland. And I soon followed.

"RIGHT THERE, BALDWYN," I whispered in his ear as he leaned over me. His massive thighs bracketed my legs as I sat on the bed facing him. Massaging my shoulders, he ignited a moan that had passion laced through it. "You're so good."

"I can be when I want to." His hands ran down my sides then lifted my t-shirt up over my head, leaving me in my bra.

Breathing heavily, my breasts rose and fell, taking his attention. "What would you like to massage next?" I asked in my most seductive voice.

Pushing me back, I fell on the bed as he took off his shirt, revealing chiseled abs, pecs to die for, and biceps that begged me to touch them. Moving his body over mine, he placed his hands on both sides of me. I took advantage of his position and put my hands on his biceps, trying not to cry out with pure pleasure.

"How about I give your lips a workout?" he asked.

I licked them, eager to feel his mouth on mine. "I think that sounds pretty damn good."

As if time stopped, he moved in the tiniest of increments until our lips barely touched. For a moment, our hot breaths mingled before he put his mouth solidly on mine.

Gasping at the heat that coursed through my body, my nails bit into his muscular arms as his kiss took me deep into a pool made up of sins, pleasures, and the perfect hint of pain.

My heart ached as the kiss went on and our tongues didn't

fight for dominance but instead danced together as if they'd always known how. A dull throb began between my legs as our bodies rubbed against one another's. The bra that covered my tits began to bother me. I wanted to feel his skin on mine and arched my back to see if he'd understand what I wanted him to do.

His hands moved around my body, unhooking my bra, freeing breasts that were finally able to rub against him. Groaning with the new sensation, he began grinding his swollen cock against me. Once again, our clothing got in the way.

I moved my hands down his body then in between us, undoing his jeans then pushing them down until his long, hard cock was released. Running my hands up and down the length, I marveled at the girth, looking forward to the burn as he spread me wide to fit him.

Pulling away from me, he stood over me, smiling as he let his jeans fall to the floor. "And now for you." He took my shorts, wiggling them off me.

I lay naked on the bed in front of him as he stood bare-assed in front of me. My heart raced as I looked at his magnificent body. "Be gentle," I murmured. But then I thought better of it. "No. Be whatever you want to be with me. Be hard. Be savage. Be free with me, Baldwyn."

KNOCK. *Knock. Knock.*

"Hey, is Baldwyn in there?"

My eyes jerked open as I heard Baldwyn's brother Stone on the other side of my door. I couldn't move as Baldwyn's arms were wrapped around my legs, holding them to his chest. "He's in here, Stone," I called out.

Sleepy green eyes opened, gazing at me. "What a great nap."

I completely agree. Just wish I hadn't woken up from it.

9

BALDWYN

IT HAD BEEN A WEEK SINCE THE RUN-IN WITH SLOAN'S EX. IT seemed as if she'd gotten over it. That was until I overheard her on the phone.

"I'll come to you. I'd rather not talk here at work."

Stopping in my tracks, I hung outside the door to her office, eavesdropping as a chill ran through me. It seemed to me that she must be talking to her ex, and I wasn't keen on her going to see him at all. The way he'd made her entire personality change —even though it didn't stay that way for long—bothered me to no end. The mental abuse she must've suffered made my heart ache.

"See you soon," she said, sounding like the call was over. But then she added, "Love you."

My heart jerked hard inside my chest. *Why would she tell that man that she loves him?*

I didn't want to jump right in with a bunch of questions. Especially since I'd been listening in on a private conversation, so I came up with something else to try to get her to tell me what the hell she was about to do.

I made a quick tap with my knuckles on the door to alert her to my presence. "Hey, Sloan, you busy?"

"Nope." She slipped the cell phone into the pocket of her jeans. She didn't dress like a shapeless person anymore. Instead, she often wore blue jeans, cowboy boots, and a simple t-shirt, her hair done up in a ponytail. Still no makeup to speak of, but she didn't need any. "Whatchya got, Baldwyn?"

"I thought you and I could take a run around Lake Travis after work today. I could use the fresh air and I bet you could too." I hoped that would spur her into telling me what her secret plans were.

Her lips pulled to one side then she turned away from me. "Not today."

Moving around to get in front of her so I could see her face, I asked, "Why not today?"

"I just don't feel like it." She went to her desk and began to put her laptop into her bag. "I'm heading out a bit early today."

I wanted to blurt out that I knew exactly why she was leaving early. But she didn't tell me about meeting up with her ex, so I didn't want to overstep my bounds with her. "Wanna grab dinner later?"

"I'm not real sure what I'll be doing for dinner. Sorry." With one swift movement, she slid the strap of the computer bag over her shoulder then headed toward the door.

She'd left earlier than I had that morning, so she had her car at work. She'd done that now and then, so I hadn't thought it was a big deal. But now I had to wonder if she'd planned to meet that jackass all along. "You heading home now?"

"No." She wasn't usually this flippant. And she seemed to catch herself, as she stopped and turned to look at me with a smile on her pretty face. "I've got some shopping I need to do. I wanna get some new clothes and maybe even a couple of pairs of new boots. I've been wearing these every day."

A plausible explanation—although a lie. "Have fun then."

"Thanks. If you're still up when I get home, I'll come over for a drink or two." Her offer only served to piss me off.

If she thought she could go screw around with her ex then come hang out with me, then she was certifiable. "I think I'm gonna turn in early tonight. But thanks for the offer."

"Okay then." With a shrug, she turned away and left me standing there.

But not for long.

It wasn't like me to be so nosy, but I couldn't seem to rein myself in. I cared about Sloan and didn't want anything bad to happen to her—especially not at the hands of that bastard she used to be married to. So, I went against my better judgment and followed her.

The heavy Austin traffic helped hide me from her as I stayed three or four cars back at all times. She pulled into a parking garage only about two miles from the worksite.

Stopping on the ground level, she parked then so did I, watching her as she walked toward the Murphy Building. With enough distance between us, I got out of my truck, then followed her.

As I went up to the glass doors, I caught sight of my reflection and nearly stopped what I was doing. *This isn't me. I need to stop.*

My hand on the door handle, I nearly turned to leave, but then I saw Sloan opening a door to one of the offices inside. There stood a man. A man about the same age as her ex—but not her ex. He wrapped his arms around her, kissing the top of her head, then pulled her inside and closed the door.

Frozen, I didn't know what the hell to do. Sloan hadn't said a word about seeing anyone. She'd told me that she'd only ever been with Preston. But if that was true, then what the hell was she doing with this other man? And what was with her liking all these old guys anyway?

Daddy issues.

Pulling the door open, I walked slowly toward the door she'd gone through. I had no idea what I was doing or what I would do once I got there. The lobby was busy, so no one paid any attention to me when I stopped outside the door and put my ear to it to—once again—listen in on a private conversation.

This is so wrong.

"How was Greece?" I heard her ask.

"Magnificent. You know you could've come to me when you left Preston. My home is yours no matter where I am," the man said. "Why did you wait so long to tell me about the divorce?"

Maybe she was having an affair with this guy.

For all I knew, Sloan was a state-of-the-art liar. But why lie to me in the first place?

She must've wanted to make me think she was a saintly young woman who would never cheat on her husband. Like I would even care if she cheated on that asshole Preston.

"I wanted to take care of myself. And I managed. I've done this on my own. I'm proud of myself," she said.

The day we'd first met came crashing back into my mind. She'd gotten her panties in a twist about the perks I was offering her. She'd told me that she wasn't going to be a kept woman. Maybe that was because she'd had her husband and then this sugar-daddy on the side. Maybe she was sick of being two men's plaything.

But if that's the case, then why is she here with this man now?

"I'm proud of you too, baby," he said with what sounded like adoration in his voice.

Baby? Oh, this is for sure her sugar-daddy!

"How long will you be in town?" she asked him.

I fisted my hand, wanting to punch it right through the door.

It was obvious to me then that she'd be busy every night now. At least until the Greek tycoon left Austin to go back home.

"As long as it takes. I'm not leaving until this thing is resolved," he let her know.

What's got to be resolved?

He had to be talking about trying to get her to be with him—move in with him, maybe even marry him. And where would that leave me?

The physical attraction that I'd felt from the start had grown into something much more. I actually liked the woman. I may have even fallen in love with her—a little.

I found myself missing her when she wasn't around for more than a few hours. I'd go seek her out just to see her pretty face and hear her sweet voice. But I hadn't let her know how I felt at all. And now I knew I'd waited too damn long.

My only hope was that she liked her newfound freedom—that she didn't want to go back to being some man's puppet—and wouldn't want to resolve things the way this man wanted to. Sloan might not have always been a strong, self-assured woman, but she was one now and I adored that about her. I doubted this guy would let her keep being the real person she'd become.

"I'm glad you'll be around for a while then," came her reply, which didn't make a hell of a lot of sense to me. "I've missed you."

"As I have you, my darling."

So, there it was. She would definitely be spending time with him and that meant less time with me. My heart pounded in my chest, urging me to walk right in to let her know that I had feelings for her, that she had more than one choice here. But I couldn't share her.

We hadn't dated or even kissed. How could I tell her that I wanted us to start seeing each other and I wanted our brand-new relationship to be exclusive?

A tap on my shoulder made me jerk. "Shit!" I hissed as I spun around.

"Are you looking for Richard Manning's office?" a woman asked me. My gaping mouth and deer in the headlights expression must've made her think she needed to add a bit more. "Because this is his office. I'm his assistant."

"I'm in the wrong building," I said. "Sorry." Before I got too far, I stopped and looked back at her. "He's got someone in there right now. Do you know if they had an appointment?" I had no idea why I thought to ask that question. But it just slipped through my brain and came right out of my mouth.

"Mr. Manning's daughter doesn't need to make appointments." Her words made me come back to my normal self again.

"He's her father?" I wanted to jump up and click my heels together, I was so happy. "That's great news! Thanks. You've made my day."

Nearly skipping out to my truck, I felt light as air. Sloan wasn't a cheater at all. She wasn't a liar either. And most importantly, she wasn't involved with some other old guy. So, we still had a chance of becoming more than just friends.

And I've got to stop snooping in her business.

10

SLOAN

My father went to pour us some brandy from the Waterford crystal decanter Preston and I had given him for Christmas the year before. "Hearing that your marriage to that man was over was music to my ears."

I picked up two snifters and held them out for him to fill with the amber liquor. "It's never been a secret that you didn't like us together." My stomach knotted as I tried to choose my words carefully. "You could've broken us up before we'd even gotten started if you'd told me about his affair with Mom."

"You know my reasons for not doing that." He took the glass I held out to him, then went to take a seat behind his desk.

Taking his cue to sit, I took the chair on the opposite side. "I do." Inhaling the haughty aroma of the brandy, I was reminded of the lifestyle I'd grown up in and kept living while married to Preston. I didn't think people my age normally drank brandy. And I'd never done it of my own accord. But when my father drank it, so did I. I'd done the same with Preston.

I'm a little mimic, is what I am.

There was quite a bit of self-exploration I would need to do if I wanted to completely become my own person. With Preston coming into my life just as I was on the cusp of womanhood, he'd molded me in ways that I hadn't realized before. I had to undo what he'd done so I could finally become my own person.

Dad closed his eyes as he took his first sip. "Being back in Austin brings back memories."

I placed the untouched snifter of brandy on his desk, deciding that it would be better to stop being such a follower sooner rather than later. A paper on the desk stood out to me; there was a name was on it I hadn't seen in years. Audrey Manning.

I reached out and pulled the paper toward me. "Dad, what's this about?" Scanning the page, the first thing I noticed was that it had come from the Austin Police Department.

"That's the main reason I'm back in town, honey." His dark eyes met mine. "They think they may have found your mother's remains."

Ice filled my veins. Even though Mom had been missing all this time, I still never thought that she'd died. To have proof that she was no longer alive somewhere on the planet would be bothersome, maybe even devastating. "Remains?" Sixteen years had passed. I wasn't sure what all would remain of her body now —if it was her. I just couldn't bring myself to believe or even contemplate that.

His fingers dropped on the far corner of the paper as he pulled it back to him. "Skeletal is what the report says."

Of course, that's all that would be left of her by now. But it can't be her. It just can't be.

Shuddering as the ice broke loose in my veins, I sucked in my breath. "How can they be sure it's her?" I looked up at my father as so many questions rushed into my brain. "Where is she? How'd they only find her now, after all these years? And why is she dead? Was it an accident? Did she not mean to leave us, Dad?"

If my mother had been killed in an accident or even murdered, then all the anger I'd had at her for abandoning me and my father was wrong—dead wrong. Closing my eyes, I tried so hard not to cry but failed. The floodgates opened, tears pouring down my cheeks.

Putting my face in my hands, I sobbed uncontrollably until I felt a set of firm hands on my shoulders. "Baby, we will get through this together. I'm angry with myself for all the bad things I've thought about your mother all these years. But the thing we need to wait on—before we go and kick ourselves for our thoughts about her—is to find out if that's Audrey or not."

Wiping my tears away, I knew Dad was right. "Why do they think it might be her?" I didn't understand that at all.

My father walked away from me; his shoulders hunched in a way I'd never seen before. It looked as if he bore the weight of the world on them. "It's because of where the remains were found." His dark eyes suddenly had bags underneath them and his face was colorless as he took a seat and stared at the paper that lay on the desk.

"Dad, you look awful all of a sudden." I didn't like what I was seeing. "Are you okay?" I'd never seen him look so bad in my whole life. Not even when Mom didn't come home that night, or the next night, or the night after that. "Where were the remains found?"

"South Austin." His chest caved in as he slumped forward and reached across the desk to take my hands in his. "If it comes back that he had anything to do with her death, then I'm going to want to kill myself for not stopping him when he set his eyes on you, honey."

Only one man had ever set his eyes on me. "Preston? What does he have to do with it? I mean, other than the affair?"

Letting go of my hands, he picked up the glass and took a long drink. My father didn't often need liquid courage. But whatever he had to say was something he had to work up the guts for. "I should've stopped him anyway. He took you away from me and turned you into something *he* wanted. He never let you become the woman you would've been with a man your own age—or at least a man in the same generation as you."

My eyes jerked to stare at the floor. I'd had no idea my father had ever thought that way. "It's my fault too. I was too easy to manipulate. I never spoke up. I let him shape me. I was weak."

"You were a kid, Sloan. Eighteen isn't old enough to know everything that a person can do to you, mentally speaking." A harsh breath told me he was taking on all the blame for what had happened to me.

But I'd emerged from the weakness. At least, I was emerging from it now. "I take my part of the blame, Dad."

"You shouldn't." His jaw clenched tightly. "The blame rests solely on my shoulders. As your father, I shouldn't have allowed him to do that to you. Instead, I hid behind some false sense of people having rights. It never occurred to me until too late— after you two married—that you didn't have the capacity to know what he was doing to you all those years. The one thing I am glad for is that you came to your own conclusion that it was time to end his reign of dominance over you. I'm so proud of you, baby. So damn proud of you and what you've become, even with him telling you all the time that you could never live your dreams. But look at you now."

"Yeah, look at me now." I still had tons of weaknesses that I tried hard to hide from everyone. "Dad, I've still got a ways to go. I did stay with him for ten years. I don't think that makes me much of a heroine."

"You *are* a heroine, Sloan Manning. Don't ever think otherwise. And that's something to be proud of. So what if you have more to work on?" His chest inflated a bit as his pride for me overtook the guilt he felt over staying out of Preston's way where I was concerned.

"So, what's he got to do with this body the cops found?" Whether it was my mother or not, it was someone, and the authorities had connected Preston themt.

"An old building was being torn down to make room for a new one. You know how Preston cut corners when he had his buildings made back then. This one had crumbled in on itself, making it a hazard. So, the people who'd purchased it from Preston sold it and the property to someone else. And that someone had it torn down. It was the work crew who found the skeleton just under a thin layer of concrete at the back of the building." His fingers lingered over the paper. "The officer who contacted me also said the coroner's report said the person was definitely murdered. The neck was broken and then the body was dismembered. It's female and thought to be around the age your mother was when she disappeared."

Broken neck and dismembered?

"Preston couldn't have done that." I knew the man. He was a lot of things, but a murderer and a mutilator weren't one of them. "There's just no way."

"Jealousy can make people do all sorts of horrible things. Your mother may have been trying to break things off with him." It was normal for him to have hoped his wife would do such a thing. But it wasn't likely.

But I knew there was no way my ex-husband could pull off such a gruesome act. "I don't think he's capable of that—even if he was jealous."

Bleary eyes told me he was getting tired of arguing with me. "Anyway, they need you to go down to the police station as soon as you can to give them a DNA sample. You've got the only DNA linked to your mother. When can you do that?"

"Now." I wanted this done already. "I'll go now. If that's possible. How come the cops have contacted Preston about this?"

"I don't know that they haven't." A grim expression took over his face. "You need to stay away from him, baby. If he did do this."

"He didn't," I defended him.

Holding up his hands to show he'd given up with me, he said, "It's safer for you to stay clear of that man until we know more. Even if it's not your mother, the fact remains that at the time of this woman's demise, Preston owned that building. He had to have known about the porch being added on."

"It could've been someone who worked there," I said.

"Yes, you're right. And I'm sure the authorities will ask Preston things of that nature when they decide to talk to him." He ran his hand over his chin. "If they haven't already done that."

"I saw him recently and he didn't say a thing about this to me." I was sure he'd tell me if he'd been contacted about being a possible murder suspect.

One dark brow raised. "Why would he?"

We had met inside of a grocery store and then in a pub. Those weren't exactly places where one would discuss something like that. But Preston would've called or something if he'd been contacted about such a thing. "Why wouldn't he? It's not like he left me for someone else. He doesn't have anyone to talk to."

"Don't feel sorry for him, Sloan," he cautioned me. "I'm serious. You need to stay away from him until things are figured out. Should I hire a bodyguard for you? I will do it. I don't want him anywhere near you."

"I'm fine." I had the gated apartment complex to keep me safe. And the big strong man who lived right next door. "If need be, I'll get my friend to watch out for me. He lives next door. And we work together, so he'll be around then too."

His stern look told me that Dad wasn't sure I was taking things seriously. "Sloan, if anything happens to you, I'll kill Preston and then end up going to prison. You don't want that to happen to me, do you?"

Talk about an ultimatum!

11

BALDWYN

THE SOUND OF SLOAN'S CAR PULLING UP NEXT TO MINE IN FRONT of our apartments had me hurrying to the door to see her. Stopping to run my hands through my hair and take a few deep breaths, I tried to look chill and not so nosy. Opening the door, I saw her carrying more than a few shopping bags. "Here, let me help you, Sloan." I hurried to her, taking half the bags from her. "You sure did find a lot to buy."

"There was a sale." She punched in the key code and the door unlocked. "And I splurged a bit on myself. I felt like I needed to do something nice for myself. It turned out to be a much rougher day than I'd anticipated."

Happy that she was sharing how her day had gone, I shared a bit about mine. "I've been treating myself too. Not that I had anything bad happen to me." Placing the bags on the table, I turned to help her. "I ate two bowls of ice cream." Stress-eating was one of my downfalls. And I had been stressing out about how to tell Sloan that I wanted more than just her friendship. "But enough about me. Tell me what made your day so rough."

She sighed heavily, then headed to the fridge. "I'm grabbing a beer. Want one?"

"Sure." Following behind her, I felt the urge to reach out and pull her into my arms, hug her, kiss the top of her head, and tell her that everything would be okay. But I didn't do any of that. "I'll take a beer."

Coward!

Popping the top on one, she handed it to me, then got one for herself. After taking a long drink, she said, "I don't know if you wanna hear about my day, Baldwyn. It's sort of heavy."

I couldn't help it any longer. She looked so worn down for some reason. Wrapping my arm around her shoulders, I pulled her close to me. "Come on, let's sit down and you can unload that heaviness on me."

Moving with me, she smiled as she looked up at me. "You're a good friend."

Yeah, but I want to be more than just your friend.

"Yep." I pulled her down to sit next to me on the sofa.

After taking another long-ass drink, she sighed. "Okay, so the first thing that's bothering me is that my mother might be dead."

"Holy shit!" I put my beer bottle down on the coffee table then took hers and did the same before taking her hands in mine. "Sloan, that *is* some heavy shit."

"I know." Her hands shook as I held them a little tighter to help calm her down as her eyes turned glassy. "I've always told myself that she just ran off to be with some man. I hated her for how she left me and my father. And now that she might not have left us at all—at least not by her own choice—I don't know how I can live with myself for being so angry with her all these years."

She'd told me that her mother hadn't been in the picture for a long time, but nothing more than that. "How are you doing with this news?"

Leaning her head on my shoulder, she whimpered, "I don't

know, Baldwyn. I really have no idea how I'm feeling at all. I'm numb. And finding out that she might be dead—murdered—isn't all of it either."

"Murdered?" This was getting even crazier. "How'd you find this out?"

"The police contacted my father. He came in from Greece to deal with this whole thing. He didn't want me to have to do it." Slipping her hand into mine, she clung to it as if it were a lifeline. "But I did have to go down to the police station, and they took a sample to see if my DNA matches with the remains they found. And I'm hoping that it doesn't match at all."

"That *would* be good." Her hand felt good in mine and I rubbed the backs of her knuckles with my thumb. "I'm here for you, Sloan. Any way you need me, you got me, girl." But she had said there was more. "What else is bothering you?"

"The body—or what was left of it—was hidden underneath a thin layer of concrete, made to look like a patio at the back of a building in South Austin. A building that my ex-husband once owned. The police think the murder occurred during the time Preston owned the building." She squeezed my hand as she pulled her head off my shoulder to look at me. "He and my mother were having an affair when she went missing. He was put through the ringer by the cops back then. And now that a female body has shown up that appears to be around the age my mother was when she went missing, and found on property that used to belong to Preston, the authorities have no choice but to look Preston's way once again."

"And they're right to." *I knew that man was horrible!* "Wait." It hit me like a brick. "He and your mom had an affair?"

"Yep." She pulled her hand from mine, then picked up the beer and took another drink before setting it back down. "I didn't know about it until after we were married. My father knew. How he didn't let me in on that is a real mystery. I mean,

Dad has his reasons, not that I truly understand him wanting to stay out of my love life though."

"So, your father knew about the affair." I was lost. "Before or after your mom disappeared?"

"After." She placed her hand on my thigh, absently moving it back and forth and sending sparks zipping up my leg, ending in the one organ that I'd tried not to let notice the woman. "Preston told Dad that Mom had never told him that she had a husband or a kid. Preston was as devastated as my father was, from what they both say."

"If that's true, yeah, I could see Preston being as upset as your father. But how do you know that's true?" I didn't trust the prick at all. "Without your mother's word, all you have is Preston's. So, you can't take what he says about the affair as the truth. Of course he'd want to cover his ass where your father is concerned. A husband who's just found out that his wife was cheating usually wants to beat the hell out of someone."

"Dad isn't a fighter." She laughed lightly. "Neither is Preston. And that's why I don't think he could've killed my mother or whoever that woman is whose body they found. He's not a violent person. The remains of the dead woman show that her neck was broken, and her body dismembered." A shudder shook her body.

Grabbing her, I held her tightly against my chest. "I'm here, Sloan. You don't have to go through any of this alone." It was awful to think that not only might her mother have been the victim of a horrible murder, but at the hands of the man Sloan had married. It was all too much for her to handle alone. Kissing the top of her head, I wanted to be sure she knew how I felt. "You come to me for anything. I don't want you going through any of this on your own."

Running her hands up and down my arms, she whispered, "You're wonderful, Baldwyn. I'm so lucky to have you in my life."

Thinking about the word life had me thinking about how hers might be in danger. Pulling back, I held her by the shoulders. "Sloan, you have to stay away from your ex. You know that, right?"

"He didn't do it," she said, rolling her eyes. "He's not capable of such a vile and violent act. I know that man."

"That was before he met you. Hell, you had to have been a kid when this happened." Time could soften a person who'd once been violent.

"I was twelve when Mom went missing. Six years later, I met Preston when my father brought him home one evening."

"So, your dad introduced you to the man who'd had an affair with his wife?" This just kept getting more and more insane.

"He didn't bring him home to introduce us." She frowned as if growing annoyed with me. "Really, Baldwyn. Anyway, Preston and Dad went into a business venture together, and he brought him over because of something he wanted Preston to see on his personal computer."

"Do you look like your mom?" I had to ask. *Who wouldn't ask?*

Chewing on her lower lip, she gave the answer away without saying the actual words. "Well, I was still younger than my mother when the two of them had met. So, technically, no I didn't look exactly like my mother—not at that time. I was thinner back then." She gestured to her boobs. "These hadn't filled out all the way either."

"How old was Preston when you met him?"

"He didn't look old," she defended herself. "Preston was a good-looking man—even at forty-two."

The thought of a forty-two-year-old man having the hots for a teenage girl wasn't necessarily uncommon, but acting on that attraction wasn't something most men did. And acting on an attraction they had for the daughter of a former lover wasn't cool. "He was wrong for hitting on you." I stopped myself as I thought that he might not have been the one who had done the leading. "Or did *you* hit on *him*?"

She shook her head before I could finish. "No. I didn't put the moves on him. I didn't have any moves. I suppose it was my mother's absence that held me back where the opposite sex was concerned. I didn't trust anyone to stay with me so why would I date anyone? Why would I give myself to anyone? But Preston wasn't like guys my own age. He looked at me with something else in his eyes—not just lust."

"I'm sure he loved your mother, Sloan. He was looking at you but seeing *her*." I felt bad instantly that I'd messed with the image she'd created of him. "Sloan, I'm sorry. I really am."

"Don't be," she said quickly. "I didn't think that back then, since I was a naïve kid. I never thought he was using me as a placeholder. I didn't know about the affair then either. But now, looking back on certain things, like when he surprised me by taking me to the hair salon and told the hairdresser to cut my hair in long layers, the way my mother's had been cut, I get the idea that he was looking at me, but seeing her. And it hurts."

Old bastard!

"Of course it hurts." I pulled her in for another hug.

"The way he would look at me—with so much love in his eyes—makes me think he couldn't have ever hurt my mother. You, Dad, the cops—you're all wrong for thinking Preston is the killer of whoever it is they've found. Not only does he not have it in him to do that, he wouldn't have hurt someone he loves."

How blind you are, sweetheart. That man hurt you in ways you haven't even figured out yet.

12

SLOAN

BALDWYN HAD HIS LIPS PRESSED AGAINST THE TOP OF MY HEAD. The numbness I'd been feeling had been slowly ebbing as he kept touching me, comforting me. And I did feel comfort. But I felt more than just that.

Tired of talking about upsetting things, I pulled my head off Baldwyn's chest to look at him. "Have you had dinner yet?"

"I have not." A slow grin curved his lips. "And you've had a hard day, so no cooking. I'll go pick up something for us while you stay here and take a nice long hot bath or shower."

"Bath. Bubbles." I closed my eyes as I thought about pampering myself. "Or maybe a bath bomb. So many possibilities." And the one that excited me most was the possibility of Baldwyn coming back to join me in the tub. Not that it would really happen, but I could have some nice fantasies while I soaked in the hot water.

He pulled me back in for another hug, this time kissing my forehead and sending chills all through me. "How about a nice bottle of red wine, some lasagna, salad, and breadsticks from Giovani's?"

"The triple meat one?" I asked as my mouth began to water at the thought.

"Is there any other kind?" His arms unwrapped from around me and I already missed them on my body, holding me, hugging me, enveloping me in his warm embrace. "I'll be back as soon as I can." He headed to the kitchen, instead of the front door. "Before I go, I'll open a bottle of wine and pour you a glass to take to your hot bath."

"You're spoiling me." I loved it.

"You could never be spoiled." Taking a bottle of wine from the chiller below the counter, he looked at the year. "Perfect."

Yes, you are, Baldwyn Nash.

A half hour later, I lay in the tub, the bubbles all but gone as I enjoyed the long soak. The doorbell rang, which I found odd. Baldwyn knew the code to get back in. Climbing out of the tub, I put on my soft, fluffy white robe, then slid my feet into the matching slippers. "Coming," I shouted as the bell rang again.

Whoever it was, was growing impatient. I hadn't given anyone my new address so I had no idea who it could be. Even my father didn't have it yet. As I came to the door, I saw a tall shadow through the etched glass—the shadow of a man. "Who is it?"

"Preston."

A shudder ran through me. *What's he doing here?*

Opening the door, I couldn't hide my aggravation as I asked, "Who gave you this address?"

"I saw it on a report on the desk of the officer who's been interrogating me for the last eight hours." His eyes scanned my body. "You were in the bath?"

"I was." I had no idea when Baldwyn would be back, and having my ex in my house would surely dampen the mood. The vibes had all been there that this might be the night that our friendship changed into something more. "And I'm expecting company. Sorry, but this visit has to be short." I stopped talking as I walked away from him then turned to look at him as something struck me. "Why am I apologizing to you when you didn't even call or text to *ask* me if you could come over?"

"Because you're a nice person." He caught me by the wrist before I could turn back around. "Sloan, honey, I need you right now. I've never been so worried in my life. These cops think I'm a murderer of the worst kind. They think I'm capable of breaking a woman's neck and hacking her body into pieces. It's disgusting. You know I would never do a horrible thing like that." His eyes moved quickly back and forth as he searched for honesty in mine. "Right? You know that I'm innocent, don't you?"

"What does it matter what I think?" I wasn't the one in charge of things. "It only matters what the people who can put you in prison think."

"If I don't have you on my side, defending me, then I have nothing." Pulling me toward him, he licked his lips. "Sloan, I really need you, baby. I've never needed you the way I do now."

"No." I put my free hand on his chest to stop him from pulling me any closer. "Not that way. Let me go."

He released me and I took a step back as he nodded. "No sex. I get it. You never were into it much anyway."

And for good reason!

I was sick and tired of keeping my mouth shut about why I couldn't stand for him to touch me, much less have sex with him. "Once I knew about your affair with my mother, it changed things for me. It was obvious I was her replacement. A look-alike. You never loved me—you loved her."

One brow cocked as he narrowed his eyes. "I loved *you*, Sloan Rivers. I married *you*—gave *you* my name. I wanted to have children with *you*."

It felt like I'd been punched. "That's not my fault."

"Well, it's certainly not mine."

The truth was that neither of us ever went to the doctor to check our fertility. But I wasn't going to have that fight right now. "Look, this isn't the time, Preston. I've got plans. So, I'm sorry that your day sucked. Mine wasn't a hell of a lot better."

"Oh, were you accused of a heinous crime?" He slumped onto my sofa, his head in his hands.

I hated myself for being such a soft-hearted person sometimes. But I sat beside him and put my hand on his slumped shoulder. "I know you didn't do this. I know you. And if you want, I'll go talk to the authorities tomorrow and tell them that I know you're innocent."

Lifting his head, he smiled. "You would do that for me?"

"Sure. Tomorrow. But you need to go." I got up to see him to the door.

One hand caught my wrist and the next thing I knew, he had me on his lap. His hand moved up my bare inner thigh. His hot breath scorched the flesh along my neck. "What's the rush? You sound like you have a date or something, my love."

"Stop." I didn't like the way he was handling me. "And let me go." It wasn't even like him to act this way. "And don't call me your love."

He didn't let go of me though. "Sloan, you're mine. You'll always be mine. A stupid piece of paper can't take you from me. I'm the only man who has ever had you and it will always stay that way. You can move out of our home. You can work at your silly little job. You can do whatever you want. But you can't give yourself to another man. I won't allow it. You gave me your virginity and your hand in marriage."

"You practically stole my virginity and we both signed a divorce decree that says I am no longer your wife. You aren't my husband anymore, Preston." I had never wanted my maiden name back so badly. It suddenly occurred to me why he'd made such a big deal about me not changing my last name back. "You think that me carrying your last name means I still belong to you."

"You do." He let me go and I jumped off his lap immediately and moved away from him. "Sloan let's not fight. I do need you. We need to make up. You need to move back home with me. Back into our bedroom."

The wheels in my head were spinning nearly out of control. It was obvious that he wanted the cops to think things were great between us. He needed to show them that he not only had a woman who believed in him, he had the daughter of the woman he'd been accused of murdering believing in his innocence.

But I wasn't so sure that I did believe in his innocence—not one hundred percent. Not anymore. I thought I knew Preston Rivers inside and out. The fact was, he'd never acted this way before. Was it because he felt threatened by the idea of me seeing another man? Was it because his ass was on the chopping block for murder?

I wasn't sure. But what I was sure of was that he had a threatening vibe to him. I'd never felt threatened by him even once in our entire relationship.

"I don't like what you said about me stealing your virginity. I didn't come close to doing such a thing and you know that." He got up, straightening his tie. "I gave you a diamond necklace that night. I gave you my solemn promise to never leave you. And I gave you my love, Sloan. You did mutter the words back to me— eventually. I never want to hear you say that again. What we did was beautiful."

My stomach churned as I recalled that night. He'd gazed at me with such adoration. Why wouldn't he? He'd had my hair cut to match my mother's style. He'd bought me a blue dress, the color my mother often wore. He'd taken me to Chateau LaRue, one of the nicest restaurants in town. "You pretended I was my mother, Preston. It wasn't beautiful, it was sick."

Making such fast strides that I didn't even see him move, a hand came hard against my face, knocking me to the floor. I held my hand to my cheek, which throbbed as he stood over me. His face was red, sweat beading on his wrinkled forehead. "How dare you! You're making a mockery of a beautiful relationship."

I wasn't sure if he was talking about ours or the relationship he'd had with my mother. "Preston!" I didn't know what to say. He'd shocked me completely. Until tonight, I'd never thought he was even capable of violence. "Leave. Leave now," I said much too quietly.

He stood his ground, looming over me as if he were ready to strike me again. "Sloan Rivers, I want you to take back what you said."

It wasn't like saying I took back words would actually take them back. "Out." I moved back slowly until I felt a chair behind me and used it to help me get up while still keeping my eyes on him. "This stops now."

Suddenly his shoulders slumped, his entire challenging demeanor disappeared. What was left was a shell of a man. "I'm sorry. Oh, Sloan, I am so sorry. This isn't me at all." Sad eyes held mine. "This is making me insane. I do need you. I can't take this. I can't take people looking at me as if I'm some kind of a monster."

But what if you are one?

13

BALDWYN

Carrying the bag from Giovani's into Sloan's apartment, I caught a whiff of something I hadn't smelled when I had left earlier. "Men's cologne?" Scanning the empty living room, I took the food to the kitchen, placing it on the table. "Sloan?"

The sound of soft crying caught my ear and I hurried, following the sound to her bedroom. She lay face first on the bed, crying into a pillow. My heart broke for her and all the suffering she'd been through and was still going through.

Moving slowly toward her, I watched her body shake, as sorrow had taken her over completely. "Oh, Sloan." Lying down beside her, I pulled her to lie on my chest. As I did, I noticed something other than her tear-drenched dark eyes. Moving my fingers gently over her cheek, I couldn't help but wonder how she'd bruised it so badly. "What happened?"

Sucking in her breath, she jumped up, her white robe gaping, nearly showing her bare breasts. Swiftly, she turned and ran to the bathroom. "God! No!"

Going in behind her, I guessed she hadn't realized she'd given herself such a bad bruise. "What happened to you? Did you fall?"

Her hand trembled as she moved it over the large bruise. "That fucking bastard! Preston!"

"He was here?" My blood boiled in my veins, heating my entire body to something akin to an inferno.

"He saw my address on some report at the police station when they were questioning him. He came over unannounced. And he wanted me to get back together with him. I know it's just to make us look like a rosy picture for the cops. Not that I even entertained the thought of getting back together with him."

My fists throbbed from how tightly I clenched them. "Why did he hit you?"

"I said some harsh words about our relationship and he slapped me." She moved the robe a bit to uncover her left hip. "Then I fell." As the material slid away from her skin, a blue and black bruise came into view.

I'd never been so angry in my life. "He hit you hard enough to knock you on your ass?" *The motherfucker will pay for this!*

She turned on the water then splashed her face. Picking up a towel, she dried her face. "He's never acted this way before. He's never raised a hand to me at all—over anything. I think it's all the pressure from the cops that has him acting so differently."

"I think you're trying to find an excuse for his inexcusable behavior." But I understood why she thought she had to do that. Taking her by the shoulders, I turned her to face me. "I won't be leaving you alone anymore. I won't let anything happen to you. Come on, let's pack you a bag. You're going to come home with me."

Shaking her head, she was still trying to be brave about things. "He doesn't have the code to get into this house."

"I don't trust him." I wasn't going to let her say no to me— not when it came to her safety. "I've got the extra bedroom. You'll feel right at home. And you'll be able to sleep peacefully, knowing that I'm right there, watching over you, protecting you."

Pulling her lips up on one side, I saw the wheels spinning in her head. "I don't want anyone to feel as if they have to take care of me."

"I know you don't." She didn't want to be a kept woman—she'd told me that from the start. "But right now, you need help." Taking her hands, I held them between us, my thumbs grazing her knuckles. "I care about you, and I can't let anything happen to you. So, you've not only got a friend in me, you've got a bodyguard now too." I wanted to be even more to her, but she was far too vulnerable at the moment to tell her about that.

With a slow nod, she reluctantly agreed. "I guess I do need someone to watch over me. It's hard to wrap my head around the fact that Preston might actually be capable of something terrible. Until we know for sure though, I think I do need your help, Baldwyn."

"Good." I kissed her on the forehead. "I'd kill for you, girl."

"I hope it doesn't come to that," she said with a chuckle.

"Me too." Spending the rest of my life in prison for murdering her ex-husband wasn't something I wanted to do. But I knew I'd kill that man if he ever laid a hand on her again.

Giving her privacy to put some clothes on and pack a few things, I went to the living room to wait. I didn't want to leave her alone even for a short period of time, even if I was just next door. My anger at her ex still hadn't subsided much at all, so I went to the fridge to grab a beer.

The cold suds slipped down my throat and into my belly, cooling it some from the insane heat that had filled me. As I stood there, drinking the beer, feeling the most anger I'd ever felt in my life, something became quite clear to me.

I love Sloan. I really, really love her.

A shiver ran through me as reality hit. I actually loved some-one, and that someone's life was in danger. Or it might be.

Sloan came out of her bedroom with makeup covering the bruise on her face. "I thought it might be better if I could look in the mirror without thinking about my ex."

Nodding, I agreed. "Yeah, no reason to keep thinking about him." Grabbing the bottle of wine I'd opened for her before I'd left, I got our dinner and we left her apartment.

She punched in the code to my place then we went inside. "I'm not hungry, Baldwyn. I'm sorry you went to so much trouble to get dinner."

I wasn't hungry either, but I knew we both had to eat some-thing. "I'll make it look too appetizing to turn down. We gotta eat. I can't let you fade away on me." I took the take-out to the kitchen then began plating up the food.

Sloan followed me, pulling a wine glass off the rack. Wiggling her fingers at me, she gestured for me to hand her the bottle of wine. "I need a drink like I've never needed one before."

"I bet you do." What she was going through couldn't be easy. "Pour me a glass too, please."

After filling the glasses, she took them to the dining table and took a seat. "Dad's going to want to meet you." Propping her elbows on the table, she held the glass, gazing at the red wine. "Is that cool with you?"

"The coolest." I would have to meet him sometime anyway, since I'd fallen in love with his daughter and wasn't about to let her get out of my life in any way whatsoever. "I can't wait to meet him."

Swirling the wine around the glass, she smiled. "He's a pretty good guy. Not hard to get along with at all."

That much was obvious, since he'd managed to get along with the guy who'd been porking his wife when she'd disappeared. "Yeah, I'm sure he is. We'll get along great." After all, he loved Sloan and so did I.

She finally put the glass down as I slid the plate in front of her. The steam made a loopy trail up to her nose where she inhaled it. "It does smell scrumptious."

"It looks good too." Just warming the food up had been enough to bring back my appetite. I came back to put the bowls of salad and bread on the table. "Here we go."

Taking the seat across from her, I noticed the frown on her face, provoking me to take her hand. With just that touch, her frown turned into a smile. "Thank you, Baldwyn. You are truly special to me. I'm so lucky to have you."

"I'm lucky to have you too, Sloan." Picking up her hand, I placed a kiss on top of it before letting it go. "This is a rough patch for you, but you've got me to help you through it."

"I know I do." Cutting the lasagna, she took a bite, moaning as she chewed it. "Yummy. Thank you so much for making me eat."

"You're very welcome. Someone has to watch out for you right now. No one can be strong all the time." I took a bite too as I watched her eating and smiling.

Shaking her fork at me, she swallowed her food. "Stop watching me eat, silly."

"I'm just so happy to see you smiling." I couldn't help myself. "Your happiness means everything to me. If you're not happy, I'm not happy."

An impish grin curled her pink lips as her eyes sparkled. "You know, Baldwyn, that sounds like I mean a hell of a lot to you."

"You do." She meant everything to me and then some. "So, keep yourself safe. Stay with me and don't wander off alone. At least not until your ex is dealt with." I wasn't going to let him get by with hitting her. "I'll have a talk with him about what he's done to you."

"You will?" Her grin intensified. "Like, you're going to defend my honor, hero?"

"I am." Her short pink nails tapped the table, beckoning me to take her hand again. Linking our fingers, I felt like a new man. I'd never felt the connection I had with her with anyone else before.

I'd loved and lost in my time, but no one had ever grabbed a hold of my heart and held it so tightly. And I had no idea if she realized the effect she had on me.

The time wasn't exactly right to fill her in on my love for her. But soon enough, it would be. For now, I had to be okay with our friendship.

14
___

SLOAN

Even as tired as I was from one of the most hellacious days in my life, I had trouble falling asleep while lying in the bed just across the hallway from Baldwyn. My legs moved restlessly underneath the blanket as I bit my lip while fantasizing about us being in the bed together.

I imagined his leg draped over mine as his fingers moved up and down my side, trying to entice me into turning over and giving him a goodnight kiss. "Just one more kiss, baby. I can't live without those yummy kisses."

"Just one more, babe. We've got to get some rest." Leaning up on my elbow, I looked into the endless abyss of his eyes. Slowly, I moved closer to him until our lips merely grazed together, causing a rush of adrenaline and blood straight to my love zone.

The sound of my panting pulled me out of the fantasy. I couldn't let Baldwyn hear me doing that. *What would he think of me?*

All the things he'd said to me earlier that night came rushing back to me. He'd said he would kill for me. And that meant, to me at least, that he cared about me very, very much. I mean, who would do a thing that could send them to prison for life, or even worse, get the death penalty, unless some real feelings were involved?

I knew we had a close friendship. I knew he cared about me. But did he love me the way I'd grown to love him? And would he want to take things to a romantic level?

My chest heaved as I sighed. Who was I kidding?

My current situation didn't exactly put me in the best place to be moving forward with any relationships. And if Preston really did murder my mother, I had no idea what that would do to my mental state.

Knowing that I had been in a ten-year relationship with the man who'd had an affair with my mother had really done a number on me. What would knowing that he'd also killed her do?

I was in a fragile place, whether I had realized it or not. But Baldwyn had seen it clearly. He'd stepped right up, right away. He had my back and that was what really mattered—for now.

I needed someone to protect me and he was the man for the job. Tall, lean, a real fighting machine—if he had to be— Baldwyn was hero material. And from what he'd said, he wanted to watch over me, protect me, and kill for me if it came down to it. Which I knew it wouldn't.

Rubbing my sore cheek, I thought about why I was so sure where Preston was concerned. Sure, the man was under tremendous pressure, but hitting me, treating me like I was his property, wasn't warranted or even expected.

A light rap came on the door and I jerked the blanket up to cover myself as I yelped with surprise. The door opened slowly, and Baldwyn peeked inside. "Sorry, I didn't mean to scare you. I just heard you moving around in here and thought I'd make sure you're okay." He came to the bed and sat on the edge of it, pushing my hair away from my face. "You know we can sleep together if it'll make you feel safe." He smiled at me with such genuine affection that my heart melted. "This isn't a come-on either. I'll keep a blanket border between us."

Or we could just sleep together, skin to skin.

I wasn't sure how much I could control myself if we were all cuddled up in bed together, blanket border or not. But I wasn't getting any sleep and I would need some for work the next day. So, I threw back the blanket and scooted over. "I will accept your offer, kind sir."

He had on a t-shirt and pajama bottoms, so he was covered. And I had on a set of pajama shorts and a crop top, so I was sort of covered. I'd never been able to sleep in full pajama gear.

As I held the blanket up, he tried hard not to look at my bare legs and midriff. But my bulging breasts that burst from the top part of the low-cut shirt were too much for him. "Um, uh, I think ..."

Even though I wasn't trying to seduce him at all, or look at his private area, I found that I had affected him. His pajama bottoms were beginning to tent. "Oh." My cheeks heated with embarrassment. He was trying to be there for me, and I was taking advantage of his generous nature. "I didn't mean to ..."

Shaking his head, he climbed into bed, moving his finger in a circle to gesture for me to roll over on my side, facing away from him. "Let's not make this weird." He shoved a pillow between our bodies, then ran his arm over my waist, holding me, but not tightly. "I just want you to feel safe, not on edge that I'm trying to get action from you."

And it would be sweet action too.

"Thanks." I wasn't sure how thankful I truly was about his gentlemanly ways. "This does make me feel better—more secure. You're an exceptionally good man, babe." The term tumbled off my lips. "I mean, Baldwyn."

"You make me want to be a good man." He kissed my cheek. "Babe."

With him there, even with the pillow between us, I fell asleep with ease. When I woke up alone, disappointment filled me. I'd been hoping to get a glimpse of him sleeping. I wanted to see his unruly curls even more disheveled, gaze at his pouty lips as he snored lightly, his cheeks red from the heat of being pressed against a pillow. But no. I didn't get to see any of that since he'd gotten up before me.

It was my own fault for being lazy. I usually woke up earlier than that. It seemed that sleeping in his arms had lulled me completely. I already looked forward to the night ahead, sleeping in his arms once again.

Getting out of bed, I went to shower and get ready for work. Pulling my hair into a ponytail, I went to the kitchen, finding the scent of fresh coffee hanging in the air, along with a sweet smell. "Did you make breakfast?" The stack of pancakes answered my question as he held them up. "Wow, color me impressed."

He set the plate on the bar. "I've got some scrambled eggs and bacon too." He put another plate on the bar then came around it to pull out a barstool. "My lady." I took the seat, then blushed as he kissed my cheek. "You look radiant this morning."

"Um, thanks." He'd surprised me once again. "You're a real treat."

"I try to be." Pouring us a couple of mugs of coffee, he put just the right amount of cream in mine, then poured in two sugar packets before bringing them to the bar. "I thought we needed a great start to this new day."

"Well, you've outdone yourself. I feel like today will be awesome." Stabbing a couple of pancakes with the fork that had been placed next to the plates he'd already set out on the bar, I helped myself, feeling hungrier than ever for some reason. "I've never been a breakfast person, but you may have changed me into one."

"Good." He took a seat next to me, filling his plate. "The

truth is that I've never been one either. But cooking for you has turned me into a breakfast person too." He nudged me in the ribs with his elbow. "We complement each other well. Don't you think so?"

"I have to agree with you on that." He seemed to rise to the occasion like cream to the top since he'd decided to become my protector. "Being my hero suits you, Baldwyn Nash."

"Please don't call me that." He dug into the eggs. "I care about you, and making sure you're safe just goes along with that. I'm no hero."

I could tell he wasn't going to let me gush about how great he was. "Okay. You're just doing what any friend would do."

"Well, maybe I am doing a bit more than what any *friend* would do." He placed his fork on the plate then turned to face me, turning my stool around so I was staring straight at him.

Only I still held my forkful of eggs. I had the feeling something was about to happen and put it on my plate quickly as he looked at me with an odd expression on his handsome face.

My heart began to race for some reason, and I held my jaw tightly. "I've got a funny feeling, Baldwyn."

"Me too." He huffed. "My stomach does weird things when I'm around you. It tickles in a way, almost wiggles at times. My heart does odd things too—speeds up, slows down—aches at times. All when you're around. Funny, huh?"

"It sounds sort of painful. So, not funny at all." I had to grin, as I knew he was getting around to saying something meaningful to me.

"So, tell me what sorts of things happen to you when you're around me," he said, putting me on the spot.

I wasn't the kind of person who wore her heart on her sleeve. Preston had taken charge of the relationship from the start and I'd merely gone along. He and I had never had a friendship. I knew he'd wanted a romantic relationship right from the start.

Since I hadn't known what I wanted at all, I let him lead me the way he wanted to. But Baldwyn and I had something completely different from what Preston and I'd had. Baldwyn wasn't going to lead me anywhere. Wherever we went, we'd go together, both of us walking side by side. I could see that now.

And what I saw was something I liked. So, I was honest with him about the things I felt when I was around him. "Sometimes I get a little dizzy when you touch me. My tummy feels like a swarm of butterflies lives there, especially when you smile at me. My knees get weak when you put your arm around me. And my legs turn to jelly when you hug me. My heart—well, that thing beats crazy fast when I first see you each day. My palms begin to itch for some reason, and I sigh as if on cue."

My words brought a humongous smile to his face. "Well, you know what I think?"

"I've got an idea, but please tell me what you think." I held my breath.

"I think all those physical clues mean the same thing to both of us." Sliding his hands up my arms, he ended with them cupping my face. "I think you feel love for me, and I know I feel love for you, baby."

"Love," I whispered as my heart stopped. "You love me?" The strangest, most wonderful sensation spread through me like liquid warmth.

A slow nod. "Do you love me?"

"I do." I'd known it for certain last night when he'd put physical attraction to the side to sleep beside me, hold me, and make me feel safe. "I've never had this feeling before. It's never felt so right to be with anyone the way it feels when I'm with you."

15

BALDWYN

Working in the engineers' offices, I'd kept my eyes on Sloan all day long. All day we exchanged sexy smiles, hair flips, and the occasional blown kiss from across the room. I'd never done anything like that in my life. I was a grown ass man who found enjoyment in playing footsie with the woman I loved.

"Quitting time," I informed Sloan as I snuck up behind her.

She spun around, her eyes wide, lips slightly parted, and cheeks red with what I hoped was arousal. "Already?"

Raising a brow, I knew she was teasing me. "We can stay here longer if you want."

Slipping her hand into mine, she winked at me. "Only if you want to."

I couldn't wait to get her back home. "I think you know what I want to do." I tickled the palm of her hand with my middle finger just to make sure she knew what I meant.

"Well, if I had any doubts about that, you just made them vanish into thin air." We walked out the door hand in hand while the people we worked with grinned knowingly.

"About time," my brother Warren said as we passed him.

"Right?" Sloan said, surprising me. She ran her arm around

my waist, leaning into me. "I wasn't sure how many hints I'd have to drop before he got the message."

"Me?" Taken aback, I only figured out she was kidding when she giggled like a schoolgirl. "So, you like to tease, huh?" I hoped she wasn't about to tease me in other ways too. I'd always had a smoldering ember for her. Now that we'd been open with our feelings, I was on fire.

As we got to my truck, I opened the driver's side door, letting her climb in. She scooted to the middle seat so she could sit right next to me. "I feel so cute, sitting like this."

"You look cute as hell." I got in then put my arm around her, kissing her cheek before I put on my seatbelt and sped away.

We'd yet to share a real kiss, preferring to let the anticipation make our first time the best ever. My lips ached to touch her, and so did the rest of me. And hers must've ached too as she sighed heavily as she ran her hand along my thigh. "Should we eat before going home?"

I was hungry for only one thing. But I wasn't the kind of man who ignored a hungry woman's request. "Sure, if you want."

"K." She took off her seatbelt and the next thing I knew, my jeans were undone, my cock free, and she was facedown, her tongue running over the head of my pulsating cock as her hands moved up and down the ever-growing shaft. "I'm starving—but only for you, babe."

"Holy shit!" I gasped as she put her mouth over my hard dick and went down on me while I drove through downtown traffic. "Thank God this truck is up higher than the rest of the cars on the road, or they'd get a hell of a show."

Moaning as she sucked me off, it was clear that Sloan did not give a shit if anyone saw us or not. The traffic was insane, as usual, and the attention she gave me had me wondering if I was fit to be driving. So, I purposely slowed to a crawl to get stuck at the back of a long line at a notoriously slow traffic light. Lying my head back on the headrest, I finally fell into the moment with her.

Kissing along the underside of my shaft, she whispered, "I've never done this before."

I couldn't tell. "Well, honey, if this is your first time, let me tell you that you're a natural."

"Thanks." She ran her tongue up and down. "I'm gonna go for it, okay?"

Shocked, I made sure she and I were on the same page before I went any further. "You mean you want me to come in your mouth?"

"Yes." Turning her head, she looked at me with a sultry gaze. "I want the whole enchilada, babe."

"You've got it." There was another slow light after this one. "You've got about fifteen minutes. Take your time, baby."

Happy to have the time to perfect her technique, she slowed down, a thing that pleased me very much. Until a series of honking car horns pulled her away from the business at hand. "Hon, you might want to open your eyes and drive."

"What a bunch of buzzkills." I pulled ahead, stopping at the end of the next line of cars. "Don't let them bother you, baby. You're doing a great job."

"Thank you." She went right back to work on me, taking me far away from the noise of downtown Austin.

Newbie or not, Sloan had me in the palm of her hand as she treated my member as if it were the most delicious thing she'd ever had in her mouth. Up and down she went until I saw stars as a rush of liquid heat spurted from me and she drank it all down without any problem at all.

Smoothing her hair, I moaned, "I owe you a big one, baby."

Wiping her mouth, she quipped, "Salty. And yes, you do owe me a big one."

My mouth watered at the thought of tasting her, but we had

to get home first. Snaking through the lines of cars, I made my way out of the knot they'd created and found smooth sailing all the way to the apartment complex.

I didn't waste a moment getting her into the house, undressing her and myself along the way. My leather belt hit the floor, followed by my cowboy boots, which I kicked in opposite directions. Her shirt landed on the sofa, her bra on the kitchen counter, and her jeans on the floor right outside my bedroom door.

As I picked her up in my arms, she kicked the door shut. "Finally," I whispered as I laid her down on the bed. "It seems like I've been waiting forever for this moment."

Stroking my cheek, she looked up at me as I moved my body over hers. "Me too, Baldwyn. This means everything to me. I want you to know that."

My heart thumped hard in my chest as I looked into the dark pools of her eyes. "I love you, Sloan. I really do."

"I love you too, Baldwyn." She closed her eyes then pulled me to her until we connected completely.

Electricity zapped me, then our lips met, and fireworks went off inside my head. Every single sense was raised to its highest capacity. I could smell everything about her—the shampoo, soap, even the subtle scent of the deodorant she wore. I heard the sound of her soft breathing as it became harsher as our kiss went even deeper. Touch was enhanced to the point that I felt as if my hands ran over silk, instead of her tender flesh. I tasted her sweet mouth, hungering for more.

Flipping onto my back, I held her as I moved, keeping our connection. Although reluctant to end the kiss, I wanted to see her face. Pushing her to sit up, I held her waist as she rode me. Just like the rest of my senses, sight had heightened as well. "You look radiant." She glowed as she moved in a steady rhythm, a sexy smile on her kiss-swollen lips.

"You look pretty damn good yourself." Leaning over me, she put her hands on either side of me, wiggling her breasts near my face.

Cupping one, I latched onto the other, sucking and nipping until she came all over me. I only let go so I could watch her as she moaned with ecstasy. "God, you're gorgeous when you're orgasming."

Lying on my chest, she panted as her nails bit into my biceps. "You're going to give me a big head if you keep flattering me."

"It's not flattery if it's true." I meant every word I said to her. I'd never seen anyone as beautiful as she was. Rolling over so I could be on top, I kept going as she gazed up at me, running her hands up and down my arms.

Her breasts heaved as she sighed. "Is this too good to be true?"

"I sure as hell hope not." I'd never felt so connected to anyone in my life. "And I sure as hell hope this last a very long time."

"Like forever?" she asked with a smile. "Cause that's a very long time."

"Like forever." I meant it too. "I could look at this pretty face for eternity and never get tired of it."

"Could you really?" She didn't seem to believe me.

"I really could." Kissing her, I took us both out of our minds to another place—a place where only she and I existed in a perfect world where no one could hurt either of us.

Something akin to magic was in that kiss; it took me under so deep that I didn't even want to come up for air. My body began to tingle all over, and my orgasm rocked me to my core as I spilled myself into her pulsating canal. We both gasped for breath as we gave each other all we had to give.

I didn't want to let her go, didn't want to pull my body out of hers, but I had to. Falling to the side of her, I ran my arm around her, pulling her to lie on my chest as we caught our breath. For the longest time, only the sound of our heavy breathing filled the room, then silence fell as we drifted off to sleep, exhausted from the love we'd made.

It doesn't get any better than this.

16

SLOAN

Waking up alone the next morning, my body was sore in the best possible way. Yawning, I stretched as I looked at the empty spot beside me. "He's up early."

I wasn't too far behind him though, and had high hopes I'd meet him in the shower. Climbing out of bed, I headed to the bathroom, but then a delightful smell wafted past my nose. "Bacon."

I hurried to shower and dress, feeling only slight disappointment that I wouldn't be meeting him for some soapy morning love action.

He met me as I came into the kitchen and handed me a cup of coffee. "Mornin' beautiful."

Taking the coffee, I leaned in and kissed him. A burning sensation began in my lower abdomen right away, and the kiss grew deeper without me even meaning for it to. Maybe our out of this world sexual connection came from the great friendship that had preceded the romance. Whatever it was—it defied explanation.

Easing back, I had to catch my breath. "Mornin' to you too, stud."

Wearing a sexy grin, he asked, "Stud?"

It must've been a while since he'd been called anything like that. "Yeah, I think you're a stud."

Chuckling, he turned away from me to get the plates he'd already made up. I came in behind him, wrapping my arms around him and leaning my head against his back. It just felt good to be touching him. I'd never been much for touching—not with Preston anyway. This was new to me. New and exciting, yet comforting as well.

"The reason I'm up so early is because my cousin Tyrell texted me that he and his brothers would like us to come to Carthage today. They want us to sign some papers their lawyer drew up." I took a seat at the bar and he put the plate down in front of me. "All of my brothers are coming, and you're coming too."

"Today?" I shook my head. "Today won't work for me. We've got materials coming in this afternoon and I've got to inspect them before we accept delivery."

"I'm not leaving you alone, Sloan. Get someone else to do it. You're coming with me."

"I can't do that." He had no idea how important it was for me to be the one to accept or decline what came in. "Baldwyn, we're trying to stay on a tight budget. If anything is accepted that we can't use, the company won't let us return it for cash. And they'll charge us if they have to come and take anything back after the initial delivery. These things are heavy and huge and not everyone knows what to look for. Cracks, nicks, breaks of any kind ... it requires a trained eye—my eye."

Taking the seat next to me, he stabbed the tower of pancakes on his plate. "I've got to go, Sloan. And it has to be today."

"I'll be fine, Baldwyn. There're tons of men at the worksite." I wasn't worried at all about Preston bothering me at work. He wasn't ballsy enough to do anything like that. But being home alone was a different story. "Do you have any idea when you'll be back?"

"Not really." He moved his food around the plate, not eating. "It's way too soon to be leaving you unprotected."

An idea struck me. "Look, if you're not back when work's done, then I'll go hang out with a friend until you get home. I haven't seen Delia since I moved out of my old apartment. She lives across the hall from where I used to live. We were good friends and I owe her a visit anyway."

"I don't know," he mused. "I'm sure Preston could find you there."

"Why would he go looking for me there?" The idea was ludicrous. "Come on, it's a good idea."

Huffing, his chest puffed out. "There aren't a lot of choices anyway. It would be a hell of a lot better if your ex was already sitting in jail. You could file assault charges on him you know. Your face is still bruised. I'm sure the cops would take him in and keep him overnight."

"He's got money, Baldwyn. He'd get out in no time at all. Plus, I don't want to do that." I felt like Preston was under tremendous pressure and that was the reason behind his uncharacteristic actions. "I know you don't agree with my decision."

Standing up, he began pacing as he threw his hands into the air. "I don't agree at all. The man hit you. He hit you so hard, he knocked you to the ground. That's not okay. That's a crime. And he needs to be held accountable for what he did to you."

"He's being accused of murder right now. I don't think adding an assault charge to that would be a good idea—or the right thing to do." He had no idea how I felt about my ex-husband. "I know our relationship seems riddled with lies and inappropriateness, but he was my first in all ways. What we had lasted ten years. Sure, it wasn't the best relationship. And now that I'm with you, I can see that there was no spark, no fire, no deep connection—it was nothing like the way things are with you. But it was something, and it wasn't always bad."

"There's good and bad in anything, Sloan." Coming to me, he spun me around and took my hands. "I don't want to argue. Just promise me that you won't talk to him at all today. Stay around people at all times. If he does come up to the worksite ..."

"He won't." I knew he wouldn't do that. "He's not that type of person."

"If he does," he repeated, "then I want you to let one of the men know that you're not to be left alone with him. And if he acts even the least bit aggressive, call the police. Don't wait until he hurts you again. Promise me that, Sloan."

"I can promise you that." I didn't want to get hit again. "You don't have to worry about me. Now that I know what he's capable of, I won't put myself in the position to get hurt. I'm not stupid."

"I know you're not." He pulled me to stand, hugging me tightly. "You're the smartest person I know. And I love the hell out of you. If anything happened to you, I don't know what I'd do."

"Nothing is going to happen to me, Baldwyn. I'll be careful. And I'll see you when you get back. Just shoot me a text when you're at the airport and I'll leave my friend's house and come here."

Kissing the top of my head, he rocked me for a minute or two before letting me go. "I'm going to miss you today."

"I'm gonna miss you too." The morning was getting away from us, as our long conversation had taken up breakfast time. "Now let's scarf this yummy breakfast down, then we gotta get going, stud."

Laughing, he sat down to finally eat, then we parted ways,

me in my car and him in his truck, heading separate directions. A chill made goosebumps rise on my skin as I lost sight of him in the rearview mirror. There was a bit of apprehension inside of me. But why wouldn't there be?

Shaking it off, I went straight to the jobsite where I found a few others had already arrived. With more and more people coming into work, I felt at ease in no time. Plus, there was a lot of work to be done, so it took over my mind, letting the worry slip to the wayside for a while.

The day went fine, with no incidents. I'd texted Delia earlier and asked if she'd like company for the evening. I'd bring some pizza and beer and we could catch up. She was all for it, and was excited to spend time with me.

Pulling into the parking lot of my old apartment complex, I parked next to her car, then got out, carrying the large chicken breast and pineapple pizza from Harley's Pizza Shack and a six pack of Ultra.

Delia must've seen me coming because she stood at her door. "Chicken and pineapple?"

"Is there any other kind?" I asked as I smiled at her. "It's good to see you, Delia. It's been way too long."

Taking the large pizza box out of my hands, she nodded. "Agreed. But you're a busy engineer now, so I'm not mad at you."

"Thanks for understanding." I followed her inside the small efficiency apartment. "How're things?"

"The usual. Tough." Snickering, she put the pizza on the table. "Working at the corner store, taking online college classes, and hoping that one day I'll graduate and get on to my real life."

She was paying her way through college so she wouldn't rack up student loans. Getting her degree in physical therapy was taking longer than she'd like it to. "If it helps you any, I think you're very smart for going this route and staying out of debt."

Taking a roll of paper towels, she pulled two sheets off and handed one to me. We both grabbed a piece of pizza and a beer before taking seats on the couch.

"So, tell me what it's like to be bossing around a bunch of men, Sloan." She took a bite of pizza.

"I don't boss them around." I took a drink of beer then put it down, grinning like the cat who ate the canary. "But it's amazing to talk and have all of them pay attention to what I have to say. I feel respected, you know?"

"Wow." She shook her head. "I don't know what that feels like. But I can imagine that it feels damn good. I'm proud of you, Sloan. Proud and envious."

"Don't be envious. One day you'll be working as a physical therapist and you'll be respected too. I know you will," I said. "Hey, I'm making good money now. And since they put me up in a place and I don't have to pay rent and utilities anymore, I've got a pretty sweet savings account. What if I helped you out with school so you can graduate sooner rather than later?"

"I can't take your money, Sloan. I wish I could, but I just can't do that." She picked up the beer and took a drink. "And I don't want to borrow any money either. But it's nice to know that you care that much about me. You're a good friend."

"What if you worked for me and I paid you the money?" Her pride was bigger than I realized. "I could use a personal assistant at work. It would mean quitting your job at the corner store though. Would you be willing to give that up?" I laughed, knowing she'd love to give that crap job up.

Her eyes lit up. "Are you being serious right now?"

"As a heart attack." An odd smell had me wrinkling my nose, and I put the pizza down to follow the smell. "Do you smell that? It's like something's burning."

She got up, going to the window. "I do smell it." Pulling the curtain back, she gasped. "Holy shit! The hedges are on fire!"

Looking in that direction, I saw the flames licking up the

outer wall of her apartment. "We've gotta get the hell out of here, Delia!"

She grabbed her purse from the hook by the door as we ran out of the apartment, finding more people leaving their homes. Everyone seemed to be trying not to panic as they mumbled to each other about the fire.

In the short time it took us to get to the front of the building, the flames had grown, engulfing one side of the building. The wind whipped and the roof of the other side of the building caught fire in an instant. "Oh, my God!" I shouted as we all moved back into the parking lot, away from the now raging fire.

A crowd had formed as everyone came out of their homes, clustering together as we waited for the firetrucks to come. The smoke billowed like a thick blanket of dirty fog, settling all around us. I felt a hand on my shoulder then it moved down my arm, catching my wrist and pulling me backward.

"Hey, stop!" I shouted, as I couldn't see who had a hold of me as the crowd was thick and the smoke made it hard to see. "Hey! Let me go!" I couldn't even hear myself over the other people.

I looked back to find Delia, but I couldn't see her anymore. The smoke began to choke me as I was dragged away. The crowd around me made it impossible for me to fight or even hold my ground.

Suddenly, we were standing by a car. Finally I saw who had me. Preston opened the passenger door. "Get in." He shoved me inside then slammed the door.

I tried to open it, pulling the handle, but it wouldn't open. He'd done something to it to keep me from getting out. And that meant he'd planned this whole thing—probably even the fire.

My whole body trembled as he got into the car. "Preston, don't do this."

"I'm sorry it has to be this way. I knew you wouldn't come with me on your own."

"You set this place on fire, Preston," I shouted at him. "Someone might get hurt, or even worse!"

"I had to smoke you out, Sloan. It'll be fine. You'll see. Everyone will be fine." He took off, tires squealing as he left the parking lot. "See, I've found out who killed your mother."

That didn't matter to me at that moment. "So what? And why all the damn drama? Tell the cops what you know and leave me the hell out of it."

"No. I'm not involving them. They won't believe me anyway."

You're right about that, because I don't believe you either.

17

BALDWYN

I PULLED MY CELL OUT OF MY POCKET BEFORE I GOT INTO THE truck. I wanted to hear Sloan's voice. I'd been a bit anxious all day. But the flight home had turned up the anxiety for some reason. Speaking to her would help.

It rang once, twice, three times and then to voicemail it went. "Shit."

I texted her that I would be home soon and she should start heading that way. My heart pounded in my chest as the anxiety level rose. Carl had been working closely with her, so I called him to see if things were okay.

"Hey, boss."

"Hey, Carl. I'm just calling to see how the workday went for you guys." I hoped I didn't sound worried.

"It went fine. How'd your trip go?"

"Fine." I wasn't exactly sure what I wanted to ask him, but came up with something. "Was Sloan okay today?"

"Yeah," he said with a little chuckle. "You can't get a hold of her or what?"

"I called her, but it went to voicemail. I've been worried about her. She's got a crazy ex that's been bothering her lately." I knew she didn't want her personal business broadcast, but I felt like I had no choice but to tell Carl why I was worried. "No one came up there, right?"

"Nah. She left around six," he told me. "I think she said something about grabbing pizza and going to see an old friend."

"Yeah, she was supposed to do that." I could just go by her old place on my way home, since she wasn't answering the phone. "Thanks, Carl. See you tomorrow."

"Bye, boss."

I tried to call her again as I headed to the south side of Austin. Once again it went to voicemail. My entire body tingled with adrenaline as my heart raced. There was no reason good enough for her not to be answering my calls. She had to know that I'd been worried about her. It wasn't like Sloan to leave me hanging either. She'd never done that before, so why would she do it now?

The name of her old place was the Heights. I'd never been there but she'd told me about it. Her black MKZ would let me know if she was there or not. But as I got closer to the place, I saw lights flashing in the early evening darkness. "What the hell is going on?"

It looked like there had been a fire. My heart nearly burst from my chest. Firetrucks were wrapping things up, people meandered around, and behind all that, I caught a glimpse of a black car that I thought might be Sloan's.

Parking my truck outside the entrance, I got out and walked into the crammed parking lot. "Do you live here?" one of the firemen asked me.

"No. My girlfriend is supposed to be here though. And she's not answering my calls. Were there any injuries?" I held my breath, praying Sloan hadn't been hurt.

"No injuries. A few people were treated for smoke inhalation, but nothing major," he said. "They were taken to South Austin Medical Center. Maybe she's there."

"Thanks." I wanted to see if her car was still there, so I made my way to where I thought I'd seen it.

Standing in front of it was a short woman with dark hair and eyes, looking frantic. I caught her attention as I approached the car. "Who are you?"

"I'm Baldwyn Nash. I'm looking for Sloan Rivers, the owner of this car."

Hurrying to me, she grabbed my arm as she said, "I can't find her! She was right there with me and then there was so much smoke that I couldn't see a thing. When it all cleared, she wasn't here. I don't know if she was taken to the hospital by medics or what happened to her. I'm freaking out here. I've called her cell a thousand times in the last hour."

"That's how long she's been missing?" I asked.

Gulping back a sob as tears began rolling down her cheeks, she shook her head. "That's how long it's been since the smoke cleared enough for me to realize she isn't here anymore. I don't know when we lost each other. But the fire started almost two hours ago."

"She's got to be at the hospital," I said. "I'll go check. Are you Delia?"

"Yeah. She came to see me." She leaned back on the car. "She's gotta be at the hospital. Please let me know when you find her there. I'm worried sick."

"Give me your number and I'll give you a call as soon as I know something." I handed her my phone after typing her name into my contact list. "I'm sure she's fine. One of the firemen said there were no real injuries, just some cases of smoke inhalation."

Handing my phone back to me, she nodded, but fear still

filled her eyes. "I hope he was right. I've got such a bad feeling and I can't shake it."

I did too. But I couldn't let my imagination run away with me. "I'll call you soon."

"Even if you don't find her at the hospital, please let me know."

Driving to the South Austin Medical Center, I found myself speeding and couldn't make myself slow down. I had to get to her. I couldn't wait to find her. Adrenaline coursed through my veins, forcing me to go even faster down the highway.

The lights of the hospital glowed ahead. My tires squealed as I turned the corner sharply to get into the parking lot of the emergency room. Throwing it in park, I got out and hauled ass inside. "I'm looking for Sloan Rivers. She may have been brought in by ambulance for smoke inhalation."

The nurse at the reception desk looked at her computer screen and then back at me with blank eyes. "No one was brought in with that name."

"She might not have been conscious. Is there anyone back there who came in that way? You know, a Jane Doe?" That had to be the reason why she didn't have her name on the list.

"No, sir. Everyone who's come in has been put into the system. She's not here. Sorry." She shrugged then added, "She may have been taken to another hospital."

"How many emergency rooms are there in town?" I hoped like hell that I wouldn't have to drive from one hospital to another.

"Look, you seem distraught. Let me make some calls to see if I can find her at any of the other hospitals."

"Thanks. I appreciate it. See, she's had some trouble with her ex, and I'm worried he might've hurt her or even kidnapped her. If I can't find her at any hospital, I need to let the police know

she's missing so they can find the man who might've taken her."
I knew I was getting way ahead of myself.

"I understand." She held up one finger. "Hi, I'm calling from
South Austin Medical Center and I need to know if you have a
woman named Sloan Rivers in the emergency room there, or if
she's been admitted into the hospital."

It felt as if an eternity passed while we waited for the answer.
I heard it clearly over the phone, "No. No one by that name is
here."

"Ask about a Jane Doe," I urged.

"Do you have a Jane Doe?"

Once again, I heard the answer, "No, we don't."

Twenty calls later, I found out that there was no one named
Sloan Rivers and no Jane Doe in any of the area emergency
centers. "Sorry, sir."

"Thank you for all the help. I really do appreciate it." I had
no choice but to go to the police.

Driving downtown to the police station, I couldn't breathe
well. My chest hurt, like I was having a heart attack, and my
brain felt fuzzy.

Approaching the dispatcher behind the thick bulletproof
glass, I was greeted curtly. "Yeah?"

"I need to speak with someone about a missing person.
Preferably someone who knows about Preston Rivers." It
seemed best to work with someone who already knew the man
and the story behind him.

"Detective Bastille can help you. I'll let him know you're
here, Mister ...?"

"Nash. Baldwyn Nash." I took a seat to wait. Putting in
another call to Sloan's cell, I felt like I might pass out when it
went straight to voicemail without ringing at all. She—or
someone else—had turned it off, or the battery had died. I

texted her friend Delia the news that I hadn't found her yet and that I was at the police station.

A man wearing a white button-down shirt and khaki slacks came out a side door. "Nash?"

Getting up, I went to him with my hand extended. "Yes, that's me, Detective Bastille. Are you familiar with Preston Rivers?"

He shook my hand. "I am. What does he have to do with the reason you're here?"

"I'm pretty sure he's kidnapped Sloan Rivers." My fists balled at my sides as pure fury filled me.

His brows raised. "His wife?"

"Ex-wife," I corrected him.

His skepticism showed on his face. "You her new boyfriend?"

"Not that it matters, but yes I am," I said. "Look, he hit her the other day. Knocked her on her ass. I told her to file charges, but she didn't want to make things any worse for him than they already are. She was at her friend's apartment. Her car is still parked there. A fire broke out, and in the confusion and smoke, Sloan went missing. I've already checked out all the hospitals in town and she's not at any of them, not even as a Jane Doe. So, now I'm here, asking for your help in finding her."

"And we can definitely do that for you, Mr. Nash." He clapped me on the back as he steered me toward the front door. "It's likely that she is with her ex-husband, but maybe not on the terms you think. People get back together. I'm sorry to have to point that out to you, but it's a fact. And we can't waste time on things like that. So, if she's not back in a couple of days, give me a call or stop by and we'll see what we can do then."

Holy fuck!

18

SLOAN

A BULGE ON THE RIGHT SIDE OF PRESTON'S PANTS OUTLINED THE handgun that he had tucked into the waistline. "And you've got a gun because?"

"You'll find out soon enough." We were heading out of town and I had no idea why or where we were going.

I wasn't sure when he'd gone off the deep end, but he'd most certainly gone off it. "You should turn this car around and we should get you to a hospital, Preston. I'm worried about your mental state. Maybe you've had a stroke and it has changed your personality. You're not acting like yourself."

"I haven't had a stroke. And I know I'm not acting like myself. When you're accused of murder, it takes a toll on you. But now that I've found the real killer, things will go back to normal very soon."

"Who told you that the body they found is Mom's?"

"I know it's hers." He took an exit, leaving the highway behind.

Everything in me froze. "How would you know that? Unless you killed her."

"I was framed, Sloan. You'll soon see by whom." He took a

sharp left and the headlights caught a sign that said we were heading toward the small town of Elgin, some thirty minutes out of Austin.

"So, this person who you think killed my mother lives in Elgin?" I couldn't figure out why he was doing this.

"No."

Since that made no sense, I asked, "Are we going to Elgin?"

He looked straight ahead, not even glancing at me as he drove through the night. "Yes."

"You're really scaring me. Do you want to scare me? Is that part of the plan?" I asked. "Did you start thinking this up right after you were questioned about the body?"

"You don't need to worry about that. All I want is for you to understand how things went down. I want you to see who was behind it all. And I want you to understand that I am the only person you can trust. Once you know and understand that, we can move forward."

I didn't want to move forward with him. But I didn't think it would be smart of me to let him know that. "Preston, what is it that you want from me?"

"I want you back. I told you that." He took a right turn just as we got into the city limits. The road was narrow and eventually it narrowed even more as we left town behind us.

He had a gun, so I kept my mouth shut until we pulled up to an old two-story house. Not a light was on in the house, leading me to ask, "Does this place have electricity?"

"It does." He pulled around to the back of the house then parked inside of an old, rickety garage. "Can I trust you not to try to run?" He pulled the gun out and pointed it at me to show me that he meant to shoot me if I ran off.

"Can I trust you not to shoot me?" I sighed heavily. "Preston, I really am worried that you're having some sort of psychotic episode. Something's gone wrong in your brain. Let me help you. Let's go to a hospital and not go into this creepy old house in the middle of nowhere."

Shaking his head, he got out then came around the car to open my door. "Come on, let's go." Taking me by the upper arm, he nudged me in the ribs with the gun. "No funny stuff, got it?"

"Yeah." Being more pissed than afraid, I did think about what I could do to get the gun away from him without getting myself killed. I'd just found true love and didn't want to die yet. "You know, if you want to get back together, this is a really bad way to get me to come back to you. I'm just sayin'."

"You *will* come back to me, Sloan." He took me up the back steps then jerked his head at the door. "Open it. It's not locked."

Turing the knob, I opened the backdoor to find total darkness. Not even the moonlight penetrated the interior of the house. "Where's the light switch?"

"We're not going to turn on any lights until we get to the attic."

Shivering at the idea of going into the attic of an old, spooky house, I asked, "Why are we going up there?"

"Because that's where I put him," he told me in an even tone.

My heart stopped. He'd put some man up in the attic. A man he thought was a murderer. A man he thought had killed my mother. "How did you make sure he didn't leave the attic?" I worried that a pissed-off killer was lying in wait for Preston's return and that I'd get killed in the crossfire.

"You'll see."

I didn't like not knowing what I might run into. "Preston, please tell me. I'm afraid someone is going to jump out and bash me in the head or shoot me or stab me or some other horrible thing."

"He's tied up. Stop worrying. It's like you don't trust me."

How can I trust you, you psycho? "I'm just afraid. This is scary."

Moving me up the stairs in front of him, he warned me, "Watch out. These stairs have a few holes in them. Walk slowly."

We made it to the top of the stairs, then he moved me forward until my foot hit another stair. The staircase that would lead us to the attic. I wasn't ready for what lay ahead and I knew it. I didn't want to be a part of what he'd done. But I took the steps, one by one, until we reached to top. I heard the sound of a door closing, then Preston finally let go of my arm and moved around me. A light overhead came on and there I saw the man Preston thought had killed my mother.

"Dad?"

Tied to a chair, his mouth covered by a dirty piece of cloth, my dad's eyes went wide. As wide as swollen eyes can go. He'd been beaten up badly. So badly that I didn't have a thought about what might happen to me as I rushed at Preston. But he caught me by the wrists before I could get in even one punch. "Stop or I'll be forced to stop you."

I had to keep my wits about me. I had to get my father out of there, so I pretended to calm down. "Sorry. This surprised me. You said you had the man who killed my mother. He didn't do that, Preston. So, why do you have him here?"

Moving behind my father, he said, "Your father found out about the affair your mother was having. He didn't know who it was with, but he knew she was having one. If you will recall, I had no idea that Audrey was married. She'd hidden him—and you—from me."

"Dad didn't know Mom was having an affair. And even if he did, he wouldn't have killed her." I didn't believe Preston. "And the body was found in one of *your* buildings. So, if he had no idea that it was you who she was having an affair with, then why would he bury her there?" He must've thought I was an idiot.

For a brief moment, Preston's face fell. My father's eyes lit up, as if to tell me that I was onto something. It took Preston a moment to come up with something else. "You didn't let me finish. You're always interrupting, Sloan. It's a bad habit. Right there at the end, he must've found out that it was me. And that's why he set it up so that if her body was ever found, then I would take the fall for the murder."

"My dad and I thought Mom ran off with some man. He, nor I, ever thought she'd been killed. Only you seem to think that." As my brain spun a tale in my head, I grew angrier and angrier with the man I'd once been married to.

He must've seen the anger in my eyes as he said, "You and I will kill your father, who most certainly killed your mother. And then we will bury his body in the backyard. You will help me with that as well. Afterwards, we will leave here, get on a plane to Tahiti, and never come back."

The story unfolded in my mind. "Here's what I think. I think you *did* know that my mother was married and had a kid. I think you wanted her to leave us behind and run away with you. But she wouldn't do that. She wanted to keep things the way they were—you were a side piece. That's all you were to her. And when she refused to do what you wanted, you killed her."

My father's eyes pleaded with me to be careful with what I said. I could see that he was worried about my safety. He didn't want me to say something that would get me killed. But it was too late. I'd said what I thought.

Preston moved fast, so I did too, running to the door only to find it locked. He hit me hard from behind, knocking me to the floor. Something was thrown over my head, and then I smelled flowers. Lots and lots of wonderful smelling flowers. My eyes closed as blackness crashed down on me.

19

BALDWYN

Stumbling into Patton's apartment, I felt as if I was going crazy. "I can't find Sloan."

"Is she lost?" he asked as he came toward me, concern etched on his face.

"I think she is. I think her ex kidnapped her." It was hard to breathe or even think. "The cops won't even begin to look for her or try to find Preston to question him. Not for two more days. The one cop I was able to talk to thinks she may have gone back to her ex. I just can't believe that." I fell on the couch. "Do you know what could happen to her in two days? All sorts of horrible things."

Going to the kitchen, he came back with two beers, placing mine on the coffee table. "Look, I know you don't want to think this way, but she might've gone back to him on her own, bro."

"She didn't." I sat up so I could explain things to him. "See, he hit her the other day—knocked her on her ass. And he did that in her apartment."

"She gave him her address then if he did that in her new place," Patton said as he nodded.

"No, he told her he'd gotten it off the report that was on a cop's desk while he was being interrogatedabout her mother's death."

"Whoa." He stood up, looking at me with wide eyes. "Her ex is being asked about the death of her mother? Why is that?"

"He had an affair with her mother. It was back when Sloan was like ten or so. It went on for a couple of years, until Sloan was twelve. And then it ended when her mother went missing." I knew the story was hard to follow and I also knew I was a mess and probably not even telling it accurately. "Anyway, supposedly Preston—that's the name of her ex—he didn't know the woman was married or had a child. He only found that out when Sloan's father called the police to report her missing. They looked into things and found out about the affair. Preston was a person of interest at that time. But they couldn't find a body, so they had to give up on it."

"Is there a body now?" Patton asked as he sat back down.

"A female body was found underneath an old concrete patio at the back of a building once owned by Preston." Saliva filled my mouth as my stomach churned. "The body was dismembered, and the neck had been broken. Sloan had to go give blood at the police station the other day so they could do a DNA test to find out if the body they found is her mother's."

"Good God in Heaven," Patton whispered. "This is horrifying."

"Yeah, I know." I grabbed the beer, downing it to help calm my nerves. "The cops brought Preston in to ask him about the body they found, and Sloan thinks he's acting so weird because of that. But I think he's acting so weird because he's a fucking murderer."

"Her father wasn't aware that his wife was messing around behind his back?" he asked with skepticism.

"From what Sloan said, no, he didn't know about the affair." I had my doubts about that too. "It doesn't really matter if her dad knew or not. The thing is that her dad wasn't ever sought as a probable killer. Preston was. And what's even crazier is that years later, when she was like eighteen or so, her father and Preston went into some business venture together and that's when she met the old fart."

"He's old?" Patton asked.

"Her dad's age." A shudder ran through me. "And what's really sick is that Sloan looks just like her mom. So, Preston comes to their home with her father and it sounds like he proceeds to hit on the girl."

"In front of her father?" He shook his head in disbelief. "Who does that? I mean, the man must've had balls of steel to do something like that."

"I know." I wouldn't have ever allowed that kind of shit to happen to my teen daughter. "I've never met her father. I have seen him once. Not that Sloan knows that. I was being a nosy motherfucker and followed her one day. She ended up at this office building and she met an older man there. It turned out to be her father."

"How do you know that?"

"His secretary told me." I wasn't proud of that moment in my life. "Don't tell Sloan, okay?"

"If we ever see her again, I won't."

"Patton, why would you say a thing like that?"

"Dude, she's with her ex-husband. They might leave town. You know, to get her away from you." He rolled his eyes. "You act like you've never heard of something like this happening."

"There was a fire," I said. "Sloan was at a friend's house at the apartment complex she lived in before she moved here. And a fire broke out. Everyone went outside. The smoke was billowing around, and her friend lost sight of Sloan. That's the last anyone has seen of her. Look, I'm a wreck and I'm leaving out shit that's important. You could get me another beer to help me calm the fuck down."

"Sure thing." He hopped up and went to grab me a cold one. "So, fill me in on the important things."

"Sloan's car is still at her friend's place. So, she didn't take her car anywhere. And it had to have been crazy when the fire began, and everyone was all over the place. Sloan wouldn't run off without telling her friend."

"What if the whole thing was a clever ruse to make it so she and her ex could run off together without either one having to face you?" He handed me a new beer. "Have you thought of that?"

"You're nuts. Sloan and I are in love. Real love, bro. It's not some fake thing we've got."

"Hold on," he said as he sat back down. "You said that her ex hit her, right?"

"Yes."

"So, if she was angry about that, why didn't she press charges?"

I didn't know what to say to that. I'd wondered about that myself. "She told me that I didn't understand things where he was concerned. He was her first everything. They share a bond. And she didn't want to bring more down on him with him being accused of murder."

Nodding, Patton took a drink of this beer then said, "She could've felt sorry for him. Hell, he might've asked her to leave the country with him or something like that."

"She did say that he wants her back." My chest deflated. "That's why he went to her place." I didn't want to think that Sloan would go to these lengths to leave me. "She could've told me how she felt. It would've hurt but at least I would know she's alive."

"Maybe she doesn't want you to know that." Patton took a

deep breath. "Some people hate confrontation so much that they'll do anything to avoid it. Maybe Sloan is like that. Have you two ever argued?"

"No."

Has she really left me in such a brutal way on purpose?

"And you said her mother went missing, right?" he asked.

"Yeah."

"So maybe it runs in her blood to run off instead of facing the music."

I didn't want to believe that. "We love each other. She couldn't have faked that. She glowed, man. Her eyes couldn't have lied about how she feels about me."

"I don't know, bro. People can be shady as shit." Leaning back, he laid his arm out along the back of the couch. "I'm not saying not to report her missing or anything like that. I mean, I adore Sloan. I really do. But you're going to have to prepare yourself for the fact that she might've *wanted* to leave."

"Who the hell goes through the trouble to disappear during a fire?" It was too much. "He took her. I know he did. And I can't wait two days to start looking for her. Maybe I can hire someone to look for her."

"I'm sure you can." He chewed on his lower lip as he contemplated their options. "You said something about her father. Can you find him and ask him what he knows about her whereabouts? Maybe you don't have to hire anyone. Maybe *you* can do all the legwork."

"I can go see if he's at his office in the morning." I didn't know what I'd do that night, as I was sure I wouldn't get a wink of sleep until I knew where Sloan was. "I don't know if he knows anything about me. And I don't know if he would tell me anything if his daughter told him not to."

"Yeah, you're right."

"You know, she did say something about her father not liking her being with Preston. So, maybe he would tell me what he knows if he thought she might be with her ex again."

"Do you think Sloan would tell him anything, since he doesn't like her and her ex being together?"

"I don't know. But I have to ask, right?" I took a long drink of the beer, hoping it would calm me down enough so my brain would start working in a rational manner.

No matter what Patton said, I knew Sloan loved me. She wouldn't leave me. And she wouldn't pull something so dramatic. This wasn't just the start of a relationship with me, this was the start of her career. She wouldn't fuck it all up over that man. She wanted to make something of herself. She no longer wanted to be taken care of. At least that's what she'd told me.

20

SLOAN

"Mom?"

Floating in a golden glowing orb of light, my mother looked at me. Moving closer, she leaned over, stroking my hair.

"Am I dead?"

Shaking her head, she smiled at me as she put her hand on my cheek. It felt warm, as if she were alive. Although her mouth didn't move, I heard her say, "You're not dead, honey. But you're in trouble. You've got to be careful. Watch what you say."

"Mom, what happened to you?" I had to know the truth. I couldn't stand not knowing anymore.

"I made bad decisions because I got bored. Don't let boredom sway your judgment in life, Sloan. I let that happen and it ruined me. I'm so sorry that I left you the way I did. It wasn't your fault. It wasn't your father's fault. It was all mine. In life, we all have choices. I didn't have to sit home and do nothing all day, blaming your father for me feeling stuck in monotonous life. But I did that anyway. And I sought excitement in places that I shouldn't have."

"Did he kill you?" I had to know. "Did Preston kill you?"

"It's hard to lay blame on anyone but myself." Her answer seemed purposely evasive to me.

"But did he kill you? Did he take your life?"

"In the end, none of that matters. What I want you to remember about me is that I did love you. I was proud of you, too. I was the one who lost out, honey. I lost out on so much with you, and for that, I am terribly sorry. Learn from my downfall. Don't repeat my mistakes. I was looking for a hero to take care of me, someone to make me feel like my life was complete. It didn't make it that way at all. My decisions took away so much from all of us. Please forgive me, Sloan."

"I forgive you, Mom. I truly do. I will learn from your mistakes. I'm in danger right now and so is Dad. Is there any way that you can help us now?" I knew I was reaching for something unreachable. Even in my state, I knew my mother wasn't really there—not in the flesh.

She began moving backward into the darkness. "This is your life, Sloan. These are your decisions to make, not mine. Fate is in charge. But you have the power to influence fate. Only you can save yourself with your decisions. I love you. I always have and I always will."

My eyes sprang open as she disappeared, and I felt the hard, wooden floor under me. Lying on my back, I inhaled, and a material of some kind sucked into my mouth, making me cough and gag.

It all came flooding back to me. Preston had put something like a bag over my head and there was something on the material that had knocked me out.

Now that I was awake, I couldn't hear a thing.

Did he leave me in the attic alone?

When I tried to move my arms, I found he'd bound them, and he'd done the same with my feet. I was stuck. Wiggling, I tried to get free, but it was made harder because every breath I took caused the material to pull into my mouth. So, I closed my mouth and breathed through my nose. I recalled what my mother had said in the dream about making the right decisions to stay alive.

As I wiggled around, I was able to get the bag off my head. Looking around, I saw that there was one small round window at the top of one wall. Dust hung in the air as a few rays of light came in the window.

Looking around the attic, I saw the chair my father had been in was empty. There were some things on the floor around the chair, so I wiggled over to find out what was left behind.

The first thing I noticed was an empty syringe. *He injected Dad with something!*

A loud sob came out of me as I began to cry. "He killed him. He killed my father."

Crying took so much out of me that I couldn't move as I sobbed, feeling hopeless, desperate, and clueless as to how to stay alive myself. I wasn't sure I even wanted to stay alive. My parents were both dead and I was sure Preston meant to torture me before eventually killing me. He'd gone completely insane.

Closing my eyes, I felt as if I might just stop breathing. My chest and head hurt badly. Whatever he had used to knock me out must've been the cause of the pain in my chest, and I remembered that he'd hit me in the back of the head, knocking me down before he put the bag over my head. I'd never been in so much pain or felt such anguish. It was all way too much to take.

But as I lay there, almost wishing for death to come for me, a face began to loom in front of me. *Baldwyn.*

He loved me and I loved him. I couldn't give up when there was so much ahead for me. Our love was new, but it was deep and getting deeper all the time. I saw a real future with him. And I thought he probably felt the same way about me.

His eyes lit up whenever he saw me. That had to mean something. How could I let go when there was something so special waiting for me?

My heart ached for how Baldwyn must've felt when he found me missing. I knew how it felt to worry about a loved one who you couldn't find. Mom's disappearance had left me shaking and crying for weeks on end. I just kept praying that one day she'd walk through the front door and tell us that she was home and wasn't leaving again.

But that had never happened. And my dream finally made me believe that she really was dead.She had made unbelievably bad decisions. But that didn't mean she deserved to die—to be murdered and then cut into pieces in order to hide what was left of her. Preston was to blame for all that. And now he was to blame for my father's death too.

It made no sense to me how Preston thought killing my father would get him off the hook for my mother's murder. It was as if nothing was working correctly in his brain. I really did think that he'd had a stroke that had rewired his brain in a way that had left him psychotic.

But then again, he'd killed Mom, so he had a strain of psychosis all along that I'd either missed or straight up ignored. Preston never slept much—maybe three hours at a time. I had thought that odd, but when I'd asked him about it, he told me that he just didn't require that much sleep. His mind was always going, thinking about new ideas and ways to make money.

Who was I to think anything was wrong with him for not sleeping much?

He also had to have certain things certain ways. Like his sandwiches. White bread, toasted to medium tan, mustard on the top piece, mayonnaise on the bottom—a layer of meat on the bottom followed by a piece of cheddar, then one leaf of lettuce, a slice of ripe tomato, and one dill pickle slice right in the middle. If he ordered one when we went out, he'd send it back if it came out any other way.

So many things popped into my head about the man being a bit off. And I wanted to kick myself for not noticing that those things were signs of him having a real problem. But I'd never thought much about it.

When I did ask him why things had to be certain ways, he'd say that if things weren't done the way he needed them done, then chaos would ensue. I had no idea what that meant and even assumed it was sort of a joke.

Preston had little to no sense of humor, so any joke he made wouldn't be easily recognizable as an attempt at humor anyway. It made me mad at myself for falling for him in the first place.

I wasn't sure how that had happened. When Dad brought him home that first time, I hadn't thought a thing in the world about the man. I did notice how he looked at me though. I should've found it creepy.

Perhaps there was something wrong with *my* brain. Losing my mother had done some damage to me. I felt so much pain in the beginning, and as it ebbed, only numbness was left in its place. Maybe it was because of the emptiness inside of me that I had let Preston in so easily. Whatever it was, I hadn't done it consciously.

I had made a conscious decision about Baldwyn though. He hadn't led me anywhere. We arrived at a mutual decision about becoming a couple; no one led anyone in our relationship. And I needed to try my best to stay alive so we could get back to that.

As more light came through the window, the items strewn around the floor became more visible. My father's cell phone lay face up. My heart leapt when I saw it.

Wiggling over to it, I used my nose to try to turn it on. Swiping up, the screen finally brightened and the password box came up. I put in my birthday, but it wasn't right. I put in his birthday. That one wasn't right either. "What did you use, Dad?"

Mom's birthday came to mind and I entered it. *Success!*

I had to get to the place where I could input a number and managed to press 9-1-1. "Nine-one-one, what's your emergency?"

The attic door flew open and Preston stood there with dirt on his clothes and smudged on his face. "What the fuck are you doing?"

"Help, I don't know where I am but I'm in grave danger! Ping this phone!"

Moving fast, Preston kicked the phone away from me. It hit the wall with a loud bang and for a moment I thought it was broken. "Hello?" the dispatcher called out.

Preston looked at me. "So, what will it be, honey? Life with me? Or no life at all?"

"Help me!" I screamed.

"Ah, no life at all then." He walked over to where the phone lay on the floor and stomped on it until it was in pieces.

21

BALDWYN

Waiting at the building I'd followed Sloan to a few days earlier, I kept an eye on the front doors, waiting for someone to open them. It was only six in the morning, but I hadn't been able to get any sleep anyway. And I wasn't going to miss the chance to talk to her father.

The doors opened at seven and I went inside to sit outside his office door until someone arrived who I could talk to. Things had simmered inside of me—the shooting adrenaline had calmed and my head wasn't quite as bad as it had been. But I wasn't exactly operating at full capacity. *I've got to find her.*

Two hours later, a woman came in through the front doors, making her way to me. Her eyes were on me as she approached the door. "How may I help you?"

"I'm looking for Richard Manning." I stood and shoved my hands into my pockets as my palms had begun to sweat. The anxiety reared its ugly head again and threw my body way off.

"He hasn't been in during the last couple of days. I'm not sure he'll be in today either." She unlocked the door then went inside, letting me follow her in.

"Is it unusual for him not to come into the office?" I asked.

"Did he let you know here he is? I'm his daughter's boyfriend and she sort of disappeared yesterday. I'm extremely worried about her. I thought he should know she's missing. Or he might know where she is and can ease my mind a bit."

She took a seat behind the desk, turning on the desktop computer. "Mr. Manning doesn't confer with me about his daily activities. I never know when or if he's coming into this office. For all I know, he's gone back to Greece. I highly doubt that though, since the police haven't finished their case yet."

"So, do you have a number I can call for him?" I asked. "I'm really very worried about his daughter."

"I can't give that out." She tapped her fingers on the desk then picked up the office phone. "But I can give him a call myself to let him make that decision."

Relief spread through me as she made the call. "Thank you so much."

"Hmm." She hung up the phone. "It went straight to voicemail."

"Is that unusual?"

"It is." She tried to call again and hung up once more. "I tell you what, leave me your number and I'll call you as soon as I get through to him." She pushed a yellow sticky note pad toward me. "Put your name down too."

Hurrying to write things down, I wasn't sure how to feel. I was accomplishing something, but not nearly as much as I had hoped. "Please don't hesitate to call me with anything you find out."

"I can see that you're very worried, Mr. Nash." She looked at the note I'd written. "I will call you as soon as I talk to Mr. Manning."

"And if you talk to Sloan, please let me know that too. Even if she tells you not to, please let me know. If she doesn't want me to bother her, I won't. I swear that to you. I just need to know that she's okay." Desperation filled my voice and I hated the sound.

"I will let you know." She'd done all she could do for me. "Try to have a nice day, Mr. Nash."

There was no way in hell that I could have a nice day until I knew if Sloan was okay. "Thanks, you too."

Leaving the building, I got into my truck. As I shut the door, I thought I might break down and cry. The last time I'd cried was when I found out that my parents were killed in the housefire.

I couldn't let myself break. I had to keep up hope that I would find Sloan alive and well. Even if she had left me to get back together with her ex, I would still feel better than I did now.

Thinking about our one night together, I laid my head back on the headrest and closed my eyes. Her skin had glistened in the moonlight that streamed through the window. A thin sheen of sweat covered her body as we'd made love for hours. Her chest rose and fell with each breath. Her hands moved over my chest as she sat up on me. "I like riding you this way, babe. I can feel you deep inside of me."

"I think you like the position of power too," I had teased her.

Her expression went soft as she shook her head. "I like what we have, Baldwyn. Neither of us have power over the other. It's a perfect balance that we have. This is what love is meant to be—shared, not lorded over the other person."

I knew then that's what Preston had done to her. He'd lorded over her, calling it love when it was nothing more than a power trip. He didn't want to be in love with her, he just wanted to have her. He wanted to call her his and his alone.

From the way she'd talked, Preston had left her alone until he saw the two of us together. It wasn't long after that when he come to find her and told her how he wanted her back.

She thought part of it too was to make him look good for the cops. But I had the idea that he didn't want her with anyone else. And that told me that he might do something awful to her if she refused to get back together with him. And if she told him that she and I were in love, then he might do the very worst imaginable—he could kill her.

Opening my eyes, I wished like crazy that I would find her today. I couldn't take another twenty-four hours of not knowing where she was or if she was safe. I had to find her today.

My cell rang and I saw a number I didn't recognize but answered it anyway. "Baldwyn Nash here."

"Mr. Nash, this is Lucy, Mr. Manning's assistant. I haven't spoken to him, but I just got a call from the police department in Elgin. That's a small town about thirty minutes away from Austin."

"The police contacted you?" My mind flooded with the reasons for that call.

"A nine-one-one call came in around five this morning from Mr. Manning's phone number. The dispatcher heard a woman calling for help and asking to ping the phone as she didn't know where she was. But they weren't able to ping it because they lost signal almost immediately. They were able to do a reverse look up to find who the phone number belonged to," she said. "Thank goodness that the phone is registered to Mr. Manning's business. That gave them the office number to call. So, we've got some information."

"Sloan's dad is in Elgin?" I asked the wheels spun in my head, trying to figure out what this meant. "How much do you know about Mr. Manning's personal life?"

"Not a lot."

"So, you have no idea if he knows anyone in that town?" I found it hard to believe that his assistant knew so little about her boss. But the man had lived outside of the country for years.

"I have no idea at all. I'm sorry that I can't be more help, Mr. Nash."

"You've done all you could. If you find out anything else, let me know. I'm going to get my tech savvy brother in on this now. Can you give me Mr. Manning's cell number?"

"Yes. I'll text it to you." She ended the call.

And I called Stone. He was the best researcher of all of us.

"Morning, Baldwyn. Whatchya got?"

"I need you to see what you can find out about Preston Rivers and if he has any properties in Elgin, Texas." I had a hunch that he was at the bottom of Sloan's dad's disappearance too. It was too much of a coincidence. "I'll need the addresses if you can find anything. And see if you can get the license plates of any cars he owns." I was heading to Elgin as I spoke.

"Patton told me about what you said to him last night. I tend to think like you do, Baldwyn. I don't think Sloan would up and leave like this," Stone said.

If I had to drive up and down every street, bang on every door until I found Sloan, Preston, or Mr. Manning, then that's what I was going to do. The Austin Police Department wasn't going to help me yet, but the Elgin Police Department might.

It didn't take long for Lucy to text me back with the cell number. "Okay, Sloan's father's assistant just texted me his number. The Elgin Police Department contacted her this morning to let her know about a nine-one-one call that came in from Sloan's father's phone around five this morning. The dispatcher heard a woman's voice calling out for help, asking them to ping the phone."

"Were they able to do that?" he asked.

"No, they weren't. I'm about to call that police department to see if they can start doing a search. I know you can probably find information on Preston Rivers faster than they can. If they will even start to try to do that yet. There's a two day wait for the

Austin police, as the officer I spoke with didn't seem to think there was anything to be worried about. But maybe a cop in Elgin will take this more seriously."

"I'll text you with everything I find. Text me her dad's phone number and I'll see what I can find out about that too. I might be able to see where it pinged last. That should help, right?"

"It should." I knew calling Stone was the right thing to do. "I'm counting on you, bro."

"I'll do all I can. I want to find her too, you know."

Ending that call, I called the police in Elgin. "Elgin Police Department, how can I direct your call?"

"I need to talk to an officer as soon as possible, please." I wasn't sure if they would help me yet or not, but I needed all the help I could get.

"Please hold." I waited while the call was transferred, and soft music played in my ear.

"This is Officer Stark. How can I help you?"

"This is Baldwyn Nash. Your office received a call this morning around five from my girlfriend's father's phone. A female voice was calling out for help, asking someone to ping the phone. I need your help to find Richard Manning and his daughter, Sloan Rivers. Her ex-husband may have kidnapped them both and be holding them somewhere in your town. His name is Preston Rivers. Is there any way you can get going on this now?"

"Now?" he asked almost as if that would be impossible. "Sir, we've been working on this case since the call came in this morning."

Thank you, God!

22

SLOAN

WITH NO IDEA WHAT HAPPENED AFTER PRESTON BROKE MY father's cell phone, I woke up to find myself lying in the grass in the backyard as the sun was leaving the sky. The way my head hurt had me thinking that he'd knocked me out for the entire day.

Craning my neck to look around, I saw two hills of fresh dirt, one smaller than the other. "Preston?"

"Shut up, Sloan," came his voice from the other side of the smaller mound. Some dirt flew up on top of it and I saw that he was digging a hole on the other side. "I'm too busy to talk to you right now."

Moving my head, I checked and found I was still tied up and couldn't do more than roll around. The larger pile of dirt had to be covering my father's body, as Preston had surely killed him already.

I tried not to look at it or think about my father. I had to do something to get Preston to stop what he was doing. "I'll do the talking then, babe. See, I've been doing some thinking and I want us to give it another chance. I've been stubborn lately and that's on me. You've been right all along. It was stupid of me to get a degree in a man's field. I don't know what I was thinking."

"I'm glad you came to your senses, Sloan." He kept digging though.

"Yes, me too. See, now you and I can start over—start fresh. I was thinking about how much you wanted us to have babies and I thought about going to see a specialist to help us get pregnant. Would that make you happy?" I prayed he'd say yes.

"I've forgotten about that dream, Sloan."

Damn.

"Well, un-forget it." I had to get him thinking about the future—a future with me in it. "Lots of people have issues conceiving. And lots of doctors make tons of money helping them out. You've got plenty of money. We could do this, Preston. We could start our family. You and me and some little babies. Wouldn't that be amazing?"

"It would've been." He kept on digging, not even slowing down.

I had to try harder. "I love you, you know. I always have—always will. I just needed you to remind me of how much I love you. Do you still love me?"

"I do." Yet, he kept shoving that shovel into the ground, making the hole deeper.

"Then let's give us another chance, babe." I tried my best to sound excited even though I was lying through my teeth. "I want to come home—to our house—with you. I want to move back into our bedroom. No more sleeping in separate rooms. That's how you wanted it. I want to please you, Preston, I really do."

"Good. It would please me if you would shut up." He stopped digging and stepped out of the hole he'd dug. Wiping the sweat off his brow, he moved over a few feet then plunged the shovel back into the ground.

A third grave?

Of course, some people who murdered their spouses killed themselves as well. That had to be his plan. Not that I was going to ask or mention anything about that.

Acting as if he was merely digging in the garden, I went on, "If you don't want me to move back into the house because you're afraid there will be bad memories there, we can always move somewhere else. Hell, we don't even have to stay in Austin. We could move out of the country."

He had said something about wanting to leave the country and move to Tahiti or something. He had at least one murder in his past he'd want to hide from the authorities over. Staying put in Austin, or Texas for that matter, wouldn't be possible for him at this point.

He dropped the shovel and I held my breath as he turned to actually look at me. "Can't you see what's going on here, Sloan?"

I preferred not to see what was going on. "Preston, we could move to Tahiti. We could live the beach life. Our children would love that."

With a heavy sigh, he turned away from me. "You're living in a fantasy world."

At least I'm living.

"Who says we can't live some sort of fantasy life?" I thought playing up on that might work. "Hell, we can even change our names. We can open another bank account in whatever country we move to. And you can get your money transferred into that account somehow. You're savvy like that, babe." Buttering him up sounded like a good idea. "You've always been so smart in so many ways. I bet you could figure out how to take it all with us. If you put your mind to it."

"The bank account has already been emptied, Sloan. I've put the cash in a black bag underneath my bed at home. I've been taking it out a little at a time so it wouldn't be obvious what I was doing. I closed the account down yesterday." The third grave made no sense if he was planning on leaving the country alone with all his money.

But I didn't think asking him about that would help things. "Well, look at you, thinking ahead. That's so like you, honey. Since that's settled, all we've got to do is agree on where to go. I heard you say something about Tahiti earlier. I love that place. I'm game if you are. I can't wait to get there with you and start our new lives. Do you have new names picked out for us?"

"I'm going to be Dax Sheplar," he said as he kept digging.

"Sounds familiar. But I like it. So, I'll be Brooke Sheplar. I like that name. Do you like it?"

"It doesn't matter."

"I want you to like my new name, babe. Pick one. I'll take any name you give me."

"Brenda," came his reply.

I wasn't a fan, but it wasn't like I was really going to go through with it anyway. As soon as he set me free, I was going to run like the wind. "Okay, Brenda it is. So, what will we name our first child, Dax?"

"You need to stop."

"You should stop digging and come over here so we can talk. I want to make up. Don't you?" I wasn't making any headway with the man. It wasn't like I had tons of energy either. I couldn't recall the last time I ate or drank. Plus, I'd been knocked out twice, and that had to be affecting me.

"All I really want is for you to shut up." He stopped digging long enough to look at me over his shoulder. "Do I need to come over there and hit you in the head with this shovel to get you to shut up?"

"No."

So, I got quiet. Trying to trick him wasn't working. I needed to come up with another plan.

Thinking about what he'd said about taking all his money

out of the bank had me wondering if he'd always planned on doing something like this. Had the discovery of the body spurred him on to move things up a bit?

Was Preston always going to kill me then leave the country?

I thought I might as well know the answer to that question. "Preston, were you always going to kill me after I left you?"

He didn't say a word. His silence told me that I had hit the nail on the head. And my heart ached that my father had come back home only to meet his end at Preston's hands too.

If Dad had stayed in Greece, then he'd still be alive. If no body had been found, Dad would still be alive. If I hadn't divorced Preston, my father would still be alive.

Guilt began to pile up on my shoulders. Like my mother, I'd made a lot of bad decisions in my life. She and I shared the worst decision of our lives—Preston.

As I watched him in silence, a horrifying thought came to me. *The grave isn't for him, it's for Baldwyn.*

There was no other reason for a third grave. Preston had his money ready to go. He didn't mean to kill himself—only me and then Baldwyn. That had to be the reason he was working so hard to make another place to hide another body.

I had no idea how I had even thought for a moment that he was digging his own grave. *How will he put the dirt over his own dead body?* "Fuck, I'm stupid sometimes."

Putting the shovel down, he came to stand over me, looking down at me, his dirty sweat dripping onto my face. "Sometimes you are stupid, Sloan. Like when you decided to go to college and try and act like a man. Like when you decided to leave me. And you're being very stupid right now. I've asked you repeatedly to shut up, yet you're still talking."

"I'm sorry." The last thing I wanted was for him to inflict anymore pain on me.

"I know you are," he agreed. "You're sorry that your father

got pulled into this mess. You're sorry that you're going to die. You're sorry that I'm going to die."

"You *are* going to kill yourself?" It may have sounded crazy but knowing that he was going to kill himself and leave Baldwyn alone gave me a bit of happiness.

Kneeling next to me, he ran his filthy hand over my cheek. "Confession time, Sloan. I killed Audrey. I killed her because I wanted her to leave your father and bring you with her when she came to live with me. I wanted to take his family and make it my own. But she refused to do that. She actually told me that she would leave you both behind and we could run away together, but she wouldn't bring you with her."

I felt sick and bile rose in my throat. "Why would you even want her to?"

His eyes darted back and forth as they searched mine. "I'm sure you can figure that out on your own, Sloan."

"I was twelve, Preston. I was a little girl when you killed her." What I was thinking couldn't be right.

"Old enough, girlie." He kissed my forehead. "But she refused to give you to me. So, I killed her. A few years later, when you were of legal age, I sought out your father and we went into business together. I knew I would gain access to you through our partnership. And I got you, eventually, didn't I? I got that sweet, sweet cherry that was meant just for me. See, I was fairly sure that your mother's disappearance would stifle your social growth. You know, keep you nice and chaste until I could get my hands on you to make you mine."

"Did you pick my mother because of me?" I felt sick to my stomach.

"I picked your mother because she had a young daughter, yes. And when I saw a picture of you and saw that you had the same hair and eye color, it all snapped into place. She was the one for me. And so were you."

Tears filled my eyes until I couldn't see anymore. "How dare you, you sick fuck!"

"I am that, my dear. Not to worry though. I won't be around to bother anyone else. You were it for me. I can't stand the thought of being the one who kills you, so I'll simply bury you in the dirt and let the ground take your life. And then I will inject myself with the same poison I used to kill your father. This will give me time to bury myself, as best I can. We will all meet in the afterlife, one big happy family."

23

BALDWYN

I'd been driving the streets of Elgin for hours and still had nothing to show for all my efforts. The light had faded, and night made it even harder for me to find Sloan. Slamming my fist against the steering wheel, I wanted to scream at the world.

My cell lit up and I grabbed it as I saw Stone's name on the screen. "Give me good news, brother."

"I found an address in Elgin with Preston Rivers' name on it. I'm going to text it to you. But first, I want to know if you've got your handgun on you or not. Because if you don't, then I want you to wait for me to bring you one. I don't want you going to this place without something to protect yourself with."

Opening the glovebox, I pulled out my gun. "Bessie is right here with me, bro. Just like always." This was Texas. Most of us had guns somewhere in our vehicles and somewhere in our homes. "Send me the address then call the police station here in Elgin and give it to them too. Make sure you tell them I'm heading that way and that I've got a firearm." The last thing I wanted was to be shot by the cops.

"On it, bro," Stone assured me. "Be careful, keep sharing your location with me, and find your girl. Patton and Warner are on their way to you now. Cohen is here with me. We're going to stay put until we know what's going on. You know, just in case anyone is severely hurt and has to be halo-flighted to an Austin hospital, we can call for you."

"It sounds like you're preparing for a catastrophe, Stone." I wasn't sure if I was proud of him for thinking so far ahead or disappointed that he thought things would be so damn bad.

"Prepare for the worst, hope for the best," he said. "We love you, big brother. Stay safe above all else. Promise me."

"I promise." I ended the call as I heard the sound of his text coming in. Holding my finger down on the address he sent, I got my GPS system routing me to the place Preston owned. The place where I hoped I would find Sloan and her father alive.

It took me to a road at the edge of town. The road got narrow as it took me away from the small town and out into the country-side. It was dark, so I had no idea what was around me, but I thought I was in the middle of a ranch or farmland.

"You've arrived at your destination," the female GPS voice told me.

Slowing down, I didn't see a thing as I turned off my head-lights to keep the element of surprise on my side. Stopping, I turned off the truck so the sound of the engine wouldn't alert anyone to my presence.

Walking as quietly as I could, I made my way to what looked like a large old house. Putting my back to the wall, I eased around the house, listening for any sounds that might lead me to Preston.

As I got to the back, I heard huffing and what sounded a lot like someone shoveling dirt. Peeking in that direction, I kept my body flat against the house. It looked as if three piles of dirt were lined up, side by side. A man stood with his back to me, shov-eling dirt. He looked as if he was filling in a large hole.

A grave!

I couldn't wait any longer and made my move. Slow and easy, I came in behind the man. Whoever he was—whether he was Preston or not—he was in the middle of doing something very suspicious in the dark of night.

I came up to the first pile of dirt. It was between me and the man, who had no idea I was so close to him. He must've been exhausted from digging. With no lights on in the house, I figured he had to have been out there most of the day and hadn't had a chance to get back inside to turn on any lights.

I took a few steps up to get on top of the pile when the ground began to move beneath my feet. It moved so quickly that I ended up falling on my ass. Lucky for me, I was hidden from the man's view by the pile of dirt in front of me.

But that didn't last long as another man sat up, the rest of the dirt falling away from him. He had something covering his mouth, so he didn't make much noise, but I did.

"What the fuck!"

Scrambling to my feet, I jumped up and then I heard Sloan's voice, "Baldwyn?"

The man with the shovel raised it over his head, aiming to hit the poor guy who'd just emerged from his grave.

"Son of a bitch!" the old guy shouted as he let the shovel fall.

Only I caught it before it could hit the man he'd obviously thought he'd already killed. I had no problem figuring out that the shovel wielding freak was Preston Rivers. "Preston, you sick piece of shit, you're done here." I jerked the shovel hard, making him release it.

"Baldwyn!" I heard Sloan call out, but I didn't see her. "I'm over here."

Preston lunged at the man I assumed was Richard Manning. Preston seemed set on killing Richard, going for the throat. I kicked Preston before he could touch Sloan's father and he went flying to the side.

Pulling out my pocketknife, I cut the piece of material that was tied around Richard's mouth. "You Manning?"

He nodded, unable to say a word. I had no idea what had happened to him, but I saw that his hands were bound and I cut them loose too. Pushing the dirt away from his legs, I found he was also tied at the ankles and cut that rope.

Just as I was about to stand and help Sloan's dad up, I was tackled from the side.

"You need to leave her alone!" Preston snarled. "She's not yours. She's mine. She's always been mine."

"Leave him alone, Preston!" Sloan shouted.

As I wrestled with Preston, I caught sight of Sloan's father crawling toward the sound of Sloan's voice. If she was in a hole, he'd never be able to get her out. I had to bring Preston down and keep him down.

Standing, I grabbed him before he could do anything else and body-slammed his ass into the ground, then I made my way to where I thought Sloan was. "Sloan, baby, I'm coming."

When I got to her father, who was leaning over the hole Preston had put her in, the urge to cry came over me strongly. She lay in the shallow grave, hands and feet bound, dirt covering her, her lip busted, eyes sunken in, and hair matted with blood. Barely recognizable as the woman I'd seen off just the morning before, Sloan had been through some torturous shit.

She looked up at me, trying to smile. "You came for me."

A howl filled the air and I turned to see Preston running toward me with a knife glistening in the moonlight. I tossed my knife to Sloan's dad. "Cut her free." Then I headed to meet Preston before he got close to either of them.

The sound of sirens crept through the cool night air, letting me know the police were on their way. Soon, this would all be behind us. Soon, I could hold Sloan in my arms again.

Suddenly, Preston stopped and threw the knife on the ground. He pulled up his shirt and pulled out a gun, aiming it at me. "You won't be taking her."

Before he could pull the trigger, I yanked my gun out of the back of my jeans. One shot rang out. "That'll stop you, you sick fuck."

The bullet hit him in the shoulder and he crumpled to the ground. I turned to find Sloan climbing out of the hole. She ran to me and I caught her in my arms, hugging her as tightly as I could without hurting her.

"You came, Baldwyn! You found us!"

"I've been looking nonstop since the plane landed. Of course I found you. I wasn't going to stop until I did." Kissing her forehead softly, I said, "You're going to be fine. We're going to get you to the hospital." I looked at her father who had laid back on the ground. "You and your father. You both will be fine."

She looked at Preston, who was laid out on the ground. "Did you kill him?"

"No." I rocked back and forth with her. "He'll have to face what he's done, and he'll have to live with the consequences."

"He admitted that he killed my mother. And something else too." Tears poured from her eyes. "He killed her because he wanted me too, and she refused to give me to him."

"Like when you were a kid?"

"Yeah."

I wasn't sure I wanted him to live after all. Letting her go, I sped toward him, gun drawn, ready to make sure he never got the chance to hurt anyone again. "I knew you were sick, you fucking bastard."

A hand on my shoulder stole my attention. "Let them deal with him, Baldwyn. For all we know, he'll get the death penalty for what he's done. I will testify and tell the police everything he's told me. I don't want his death on your conscience." She turned to look at her father. "I'm just so damn glad to see Dad alive that I don't want anyone to die. Not tonight."

The cops pulled up, the sound of officers coming around back telling I should holster my gun and let them take care of Preston. "You got it. I love you."

"I love you too. Now, can you take me home?" She went limp in my arms and I picked her up, carrying her to the nearest ambulance.

24

SLOAN

"Here you go," the nurse said as she started the morphine drip. "This isn't enough to knock you out, but just enough to take the edge off the pain, Mrs. Rivers."

"Sloan," I said quickly. "I never want to be called Mrs. Rivers again."

"Sorry." Her lips formed a thin line. "Sloan, this will administer a tiny drip through your IV every half hour. If you begin to feel any pain before that, just buzz me and I'll shorten the length between drips."

Baldwyn came into my hospital room, carrying a crystal vase full of a variety of pink and yellow flowers. "I see you've been made comfortable."

A warm feeling came over me and a smile formed on my newly stitched lips. "Oh yeah, that's the good stuff right there, nursey-poo." I looked at the tube beside me, thankful for the powerful drug that took away all my pain, angst, and worry. "I think you're my new best friend."

"You're not the first person to say that," the nurse said as she headed to the door. She stopped to talk to Baldwyn. "If you see her experiencing any pain, please push the nurses' button on the right-side rail of her bed and I'll come see what's up."

"Will do. Now that I've handled the paperwork and billing, I'm not leaving this lady's side." He patted her on the back. "Thanks for taking care of my girl. I've got Anne's Pastries catering breakfast for the nurses' station for you guys this morning as a thank you for taking such good care of Sloan and her father."

The nurse turned to look at me with a wide grin on her face. "Now this one is a keeper, Sloan. Don't let him slip through your fingers." She looked back at Baldwyn. "Thank you, Mr. Nash. We all appreciate you thinking about us."

She left us alone and Baldwyn stood there, looking at me with a smile. "Four stitches on your lips. Ten staples on the gashes on the back of your head. And remarkably no internal injuries. You are one tough cookie." He came to sit on the bed next to me, resting his hand on my shoulder. "You look sleepy. Get some rest. I'll be here when you wake up."

"No. I don't want to close my eyes. I don't like what comes up when my mind rests." I was chilled out with the morphine, but I wasn't completely at ease. "It seems that my mother wants to come to me in my dreams lately. I'd rather not think of her as dead until I know for sure."

"I understand that. But you need to rest so you'll heal faster." Caressing my cheek, he gazed into my eyes. "With the nutrients they've given you through the IV, your eyes already look a lot better."

"I feel better." When Baldwyn first put me into the back of the ambulance, I'd felt worse than I ever had before in my life. "I still can't believe you were able to find us way out there in the boonies."

"It was a team effort. I had Stone researching things for me.

He's great at that kind of thing." Kissing my forehead, he sighed softly. "I'm just so thankful I found you in time."

Cradling his face between my hands, I was grateful for more than just that. "I'm grateful for my father. I'd already accepted his death. You came along and miracles happened, Baldwyn Nash—my hero."

"I'd do anything for you—anything and everything. I'm glad your dad made it too." He pulled back, taking a seat on the edge of my bed. "I'm not so sure how happy I am about Preston making it though. If he somehow squirms out of this, I don't know what I'll do."

Even with the medication to soothe me, just thinking about what Preston had done to me and my entire family made me sick. "He's an extremely disturbed man. And I'm sure that karma will deal with him fairly. He took my mother's life and he took mine in a way too. He stole both of us from my father. The worst thing to me was that he'd planned it all. There was never love in anything he did. There was only some sick, twisted plan and everything he did was for that plan—not me, not my mother, just his horrifying plan to have us both."

"I saw a cop sitting outside a door down the hallway," Baldwyn said with a frown. "I guess that means he made it through the surgery to repair his shoulder. I have to admit I was hoping he wouldn't make it."

I didn't know what I hoped for. "I'm just glad this is all over. I mean, except for knowing if that body is Mom's or not. But Preston's confession pretty much wraps that up." Thinking of my mother's neck being broken, then her body hacked into pieces, bothered me to no end. And so did the fact that I'd fallen for Preston and his lies. "I'm going to need help to get past what's happened to me."

Taking my hand, he held it to his heart. "And you will get all the help you need for as long as you need it. My treat." He kissed the top of my hand. "I'll be here for you forever, my love—forever and ever."

"If you want to help me, don't offer to take care of me." I wasn't sure if I could ever find it in me to trust anyone again. "I've got to do this on my own. I've got money. I've still got my career. He didn't take away my ability to take care of myself. But he did take my ability to fully trust people."

As he looked at the floor, I watched Baldwyn take the blow I hadn't meant to deliver so harshly. "I can see why you feel that way and I don't blame you for it. I won't jump in and try to take away your independence. But I am here for you in any capacity that you need me to be. If you feel that you need to take time off to adjust to things, you can have it."

"I'm not about to flake on my first job, Baldwyn. I can do my job. I can live my life. But there will be some changes." How could there not be? "My mother wasn't exactly the villain I made her out to be all these years. She was protecting me and that's why he killed her. She came to me in a dream and told me that she'd made choices that led to her death. But did she really make them, or did Preston manipulate her into making them?" I wasn't sure about anything anymore. "He certainly manipulated me into having a relationship with him, into getting married. Only I never saw it for what it was. I never even thought for a moment that I wasn't in charge of the decisions I made. But I was wrong. And for all I know, I've been wrong about everything my entire life."

Getting up, Baldwyn walked across the room to look out the window as the sun started to come up. "Well, yesterday is gone—thank God. This is a new day and you can start over again. You've got me in your corner, Sloan." He turned to face me, pulling the curtain back to let the light stream into the room. "I know you're thinking that you've been living a lie—at least the part of your life that you spent with him. This—what you and I have—this is no lie."

How I wish I could believe that.

"Time, Baldwyn," I whispered. I knew what I said hurt him. "I'll need time, patience, and your word that you'll do as I ask you to if I feel I need space." I had no idea what I would need, but I wanted to be sure I didn't have to fight him if I felt I needed to be alone for a while.

"Space," he murmured. Nodding, he said, "I told you that I would give you anything and everything you want, and I meant that. If you need space, then I will give you that. Just promise not to shut me out completely. I do love you and I care about you. And maybe you'll find that love you had for me buried underneath the rubble that man made out of your heart."

My heart did feel like a pile of debris. "Thank you. It means a lot to me to have you understand what I've been through. What I'll be going through for God knows how long."

Baldwyn was thirty-five, not old but not young either. He was at his prime, physically and mentally. Any woman would be lucky to have him. And I had no right to ask him to hang on to what we had when I had no idea if I could ever get back to the person I was before I found out how profoundly I'd been brainfucked.

"Will you be going home with me?" he asked as he looked out the window at the rising sun.

"I think I should go to my place. It's right next door to you. But it'll give us some breathing room."

"I don't need any breathing room." I could tell how much this hurt him. "But I know that you do. My door will always be open for you. You know, just in case you want me in the middle of the night or something like that."

I chuckled a little. "You'd be my booty-call, Baldwyn?"

"I'll be anything you need me to be." He turned and came to sit in the chair next to my bed.

I didn't know what to say. I was sorry for everything. It wasn't his fault that Preston had screwed me up. It wasn't his fault that we'd fallen for each other and then I was dealt a shitty hand that ruined what we'd found. "Friends, no matter what, right?"

"Friends to the end," he assured me.

"Thank you." He had no idea how much it meant to hear him say that. "I need your friendship more than I need anything else right now."

"No problem. You've got that and always will, Sloan."

25

BALDWYN

Sloan finally fell into what looked like a peaceful sleep once night fell. I knew so much was going on in her mind and prayed that once she began to heal, the lack of trust she now felt would begin to fade. She would need therapy to get past what Preston had done to her and her family, but at least there was something that could help her.

Playing a game on my phone, I sat in the chair beside her bed, not quite ready to sleep just yet. I'd been awake for two days so I was afraid that when I fell asleep, I would sleep like a dead man. Something told me not to take Sloan's safety for granted. Plus, I figured they'd let her go home the next morning since her injuries had been dealt with. I could sleep then— my brothers would be around to make sure Sloan was safe.

A large part of me felt wounded by the distrust I saw in Sloan's eyes—even distrust for me. I couldn't blame her for feeling that way though. Preston's manipulations were astronomical. Anyone would've felt the same way Sloan did after finding out just how much she'd been duped by the man.

I'd never been in a hospital for any longer than to visit a couple of friends once or twice. The daytime was busy, noisy even. But after dinner was served and the plates picked back up by the cafeteria staff, the place went quiet—an eerie quiet.

The number of nurses was cut in half, as the patients would all sleep until morning. I got up to go look out into the hallway, just to see how many people were out there.

A blue light came off the computer screen at the nurses' station, but no one was there. They must've been elsewhere, doing the things night nurses had to do. The lights had been turned off in the hall. Only tiny, dim lights ran along the bottom of the walls on both sides.

Squinting, I wasn't sure if I saw anyone sitting outside the door of what I believed was Preston's room. The cop who was guarding him could've been slumped over, sleeping. Or they might've even moved Preston out of the hospital and into an infirmary at the jail.

An uneasy feeling came over me and I looked back at Sloan as her chest rose and fell in a slow, constant motion. I felt like I should go down to the room to check things out. Maybe even wake the cop up if he had fallen asleep.

But leaving her alone felt wrong, so I minded my own business and went back into her room, taking my seat and going back to playing the game on my cell phone. I had to trust in the police to take care of Preston. But I had an idea about how Sloan felt. It was hard to trust anyone where that man was concerned.

Putting the phone down, I took a moment to look into my own feelings. Sloan had been manipulated for years. Maybe she and I hadn't connected in an entirely natural way at all. Maybe she saw something in me that reminded her of her ex. Or maybe I was the complete opposite—which I hoped was the truth.

What if Sloan never really loved me?

What if Sloan didn't know how to love? What if she was incapable of loving anyone, due to how her brain had been messed with so completely? And what would that mean for us?

I knew I loved the woman as she was. But would I love the woman she would become?

The events and revelations of the last couple days would almost certainly radically change her. Something this deep and profound had to change a person. There was no way it couldn't.

She'd carry emotional scars forever. Maybe even the best psychologists in the world wouldn't be able to mend her poor mind. What would I do then?

Looking at her, her stitched up lips pouting as she slept, my heart melted. *I love her. I really, really love her.*

No matter how she changed, I instinctively knew that I would never stop loving her. The bond I had with her was strong. It felt unbreakable.

If I had to get therapy to help understand Sloan, then I'd get it. I wouldn't leave her alone in her fight to get mentally healthy. Even if she asked me to leave her alone, I would only be a phone call away when she needed me.

My ears pricked as I heard soft footsteps coming down the hallway. The sounds were too soft, as if the person wore socks and not shoes. No nurse would be padding around in socks, or at least I thought none would.

But who was I to say?

I went back to playing my game so I would stop thinking so much about things that were out of my control anyway.

My eyes were drawn away from my phone screen as the door slowly opened. I figured it was a nurse there to check on Sloan, but when the door opened a bit more, I saw that it wasn't a nurse at all. The hospital gown moved around the knees of the person who was coming into the room. Hairy legs, yellow booties covering his feet, and a gun in his hand. Preston.

"You," he growled. "Why are you here with her? She isn't yours, you fucking prick."

I had nothing on me to protect her with. The hospital had

stiff rules about bringing guns in the hospital. Preston must've gotten the one he was holding off the cop that had been guarding him.

"So, you've killed a cop now, Preston? Do you think that's a smart thing to do? I mean, you've got the murder charge to face for killing Sloan's mother. You've got two kidnapping charges and attempted murder charges from what you did to Sloan and her father. You've probably got even more coming once the district attorney gets your file. Adding in something to do with fucking with a policeman is sure to get you the death penalty."

"You don't seem to realize that I don't plan to go to jail or face any jury of my peers, you fuck-tard." His hand shook as he held the gun up, pointing it at me.

I'd shot him in the right shoulder for a good reason. I'd noticed that he held the knife in his right hand, making him righthanded. Holding the gun wasn't an easy chore for the injured man. "How many stitches did it take to close up the holes I made in your shoulder, Preston? Ten, fifteen, twenty?"

"Fuck off, jackass." He moved into the room, the door closing softly behind him. "You weren't going to be a part of this. Since you've decided to hang around, you'll join us all in the afterlife. Only you won't be a part of what we'll share. Audrey, Sloan, and I will be together for eternity soon."

"You're most definitely going to hell," I let him know. "I don't know if you thought about that or not, but you won't be in Heaven with either Sloan or her mother. Murder victims always go to Heaven, Preston. Murderers always go to hell. It's just the way it goes." Stalling him with my theories of the afterlife, I knew I had to come up with something to keep him from shooting anyone until I found some kind of weapon of my own. So far, I hadn't seen a single item in the room that I could use.

Leaning against the wall, he showed signs that the walk to Sloan's room had taken a toll on him. I was sure the nurses had given him something to help him sleep too, and something for the pain. The room was probably spinning for him. "You don't know shit. I don't know what she sees in you. But that won't matter anyway. Maybe I won't kill you. Maybe I don't want to chance having to deal with your ass on the other side."

"You're really crazy, you know that? Sloan told me about your sick plan. So, did you entice her mother into having an affair with you or what?"

"I spotted Audrey at the grocery store. She was buying copious amounts of wine. I saw the wedding ring on her finger and knew immediately that her marriage was on the rocks. No happily married woman drinks that much alcohol. But that wasn't going to be enough for me. I wanted a woman with a daughter. A daughter who resembled her, so I could have the best of both worlds. The older, mature, experienced version, and the young, fresh, virginal version."

"How'd you do it, Preston?" I had to keep him talking to distract him. "How'd you get Audrey to do what you wanted her to?"

"I followed her through the store until we *accidentally* ran into each other when we both went to grab a carton of eggs." Smirking, he seemed proud of himself. "I asked her how she was doing, and she huffed and said she was doing okay. I really wanted to know if she had a daughter, so I asked if her kids were getting her down. She said she only had one kid, a girl in fifth grade who wasn't any problem at all. That made me incredibly happy. So, I went one step further, asking if life was getting her down. She was quick to say that married life wasn't all it's cracked up to be. And from there we went to lunch, grabbed some drinks at a nearby bar, then headed to a motel to finish the deed. She cried afterward, saying she didn't know what made her do what she'd done."

"Let me guess, you put something in her drink."

"At lunch, yes. A little ecstasy was all it took to get her to loosen up and give into me. But Audrey proved harder to manipulate than I thought she'd be. Even with the drugs I fed her, she wouldn't bring her daughter to me. Not that I told her what I wanted with the girl. I wasn't going to be honest about that." He grinned, clearly thinking he was the smartest man in the world.

"You wanted Audrey to think that you wanted to take care of her and her little girl." I could see right through him. And it occurred to me that Audrey may have begun seeing through him, and that's why she wouldn't bring her daughter around him. "She was too smart for you."

"She was," he agreed. "But, when all was said and done, I ended her anyway. And I got her daughter. Sure, I had to wait a few years, but I was the one who had the first taste of her. It was a nice consolation prize. And now, I will take her life, then my own, and you can sit there and play the role of the witness in this whole thing. You can tell everyone what I've said, and you'll become some sort of a hero for doing it too."

"I'm not cool with any of that, Preston." Sloan began to stir, as Preston had begun to raise his voice. I put my hand on hers, stroking it to lull her back to sleep. I didn't want any more bad memories to lurk in her poor tortured mind.

It was becoming obvious to me that I would have to use the only weapon I had—my strength—to get the gun away from the insane man. But just as I was about to jump up and make my move, the door flew open, hitting Preston in the face as he'd been leaning on the wall.

Frozen in place, I saw another man in a hospital gown come into the room, holding something shiny over his head. Preston stumbled forward as the door bounced off him, then slammed shut again. "What the fuck?"

Sloan's father must've heard Preston's voice as he was resting in the room next door. He slammed what looked like a stainless-steel bedpan down on Preston's head. "Fuck you, Preston Rivers!"

Sloan sat up in bed with fear in her eyes. "Dad?"

The gun slid across the floor and I dove for it as Preston crumbled to the floor in an unconscious heap. I grabbed the gun, pointing it at him. "You okay, Richard?"

He slumped into the chair I'd vacated, pale and shaking. The bedpan made a hellacious sound as it fell from his hand, landing on the floor. "I think I am. Sloan, honey, will you press the button to call the nurse?"

"What the hell happened?" she asked as she pressed the button.

"He came back to finish the job," I told her. "I should probably just shoot him now."

The door opened and two male nurses came in. "No, you shouldn't," one of them said as the other held his hand out for the gun.

I placed it in his hand, then went to stand on the other side of Sloan. "I guess that's a no."

While one of the nurses saw to Preston, the other came to Sloan. "Mrs. Rivers, are you okay?"

Sloan reached out to me and I gave her my hand. She looked up at me with tears rolling down her cheeks. "Can you do me a favor and change my last name?"

Is that a marriage proposal?

26

SLOAN

Dad had to stay a few more days in the hospital, as the poison Preston had injected into him had done some internal damage that had to be monitored. But the doctors expected a full recovery. I got to go home after spending one night in the hospital. Even the doctors thought I'd get more rest being at home than there.

It was decided that if Preston had enough strength to overpower a cop, take his gun, shoot him with it, then walk down a long hall to shoot me, that he was strong enough to go to county jail to await his trial. The judge hadn't set bail yet, but it was expected to be too high for him to pay.

I told the authorities about how Preston had told me he'd closed his bank account and that his cash was in a black bag under his bed. That gave Preston no access to his money, as they went to retrieve it from his home. While they were there, they also did a thorough inspection of his home to see if they could find any more evidence that would help put him away for a long, long time.

Baldwyn's brothers stood on the sidewalk as we pulled up. Seeing the smiles on all their faces, I couldn't help feeling like I was part of their family somehow. Patton came to open the passenger door for me. "Welcome back." Pulling me out of the truck, he wrapped his arms around me, hugging me tight. "We're so glad to see you, you have no idea."

As soon as he let me go, another brother scooped me up and they passed me along from one to another until I ended up standing at Baldwyn's front door. He held it open for me. "I'm hoping you'll stay with me for a bit. It might sound crazy, but until Preston is in prison, I don't want to let my guard down where you're concerned."

"Think he'll bust out of the hoosegow?" I laughed, but there was a niggling fear that he might do just that.

"Yep," Baldwyn said as he took my hand, leading me inside.

"Yeah, me too." I'd never thought Preston was capable of any of the things he'd done. Breaking out of jail wasn't beyond the realm of possibilities.

Just as I settled on the sofa, the doorbell rang. Cohen smiled as he went to answer the door. "Now, I wonder who this could be."

"Me too." I thought everyone was already there. Unless they had everyone from work coming by to see me. Which I hoped wasn't the case.

As soon as he opened the door, Delia came in with tears in her eyes. "Oh, Sloan! It's so good to see you."

I got up as she held her arms out to me and our embrace lasted a long time. She couldn't find the words to say how worried she'd been about me. "I'm sorry I worried you," I finally said.

"I'm sorry I didn't notice you'd been kidnapped." She held my hand as we sat down next to each other on the sofa. "What kind of a friend doesn't realize her friend is missing until an hour has passed?"

"One who's in the middle of a crisis with smoke making it

impossible to see what's going on." Preston had really outdone himself with all his antics. "I'm sorry that my presence there caused so much destruction. Baldwyn told me that no one was hurt, which I'm thankful for."

"Yes, thank the lord above." Patting the hand she held, she looked as if she had something to tell me.

"What's wrong, Delia?"

"Your car, Sloan. The paint is peeling because it was parked so close to the fire. And the front tires kind of melted too. I know you loved that car ..."

I stopped her before she could go on. "I don't ever want to see that car. He gave it to me, and I want no reminders of him." I looked over my shoulder to find Baldwyn. "Can you deal with the car? I want to give it to a charity or something. And I never want to see it or anything I had in it again."

"I'll handle that," he assured me. "Should I also handle getting you something else to drive? I don't mind."

Looking at Delia, I had an idea. "Do you still want to be my personal assistant?"

The way her eyes lit up told me she was still interested in the position. "You mean that's still an option?"

"Of course it is." I wanted to get her started on the job ASAP. "First order of business: tell the corner store that you quit. Second order of business: I'm going to put you in charge of finding me a new car. And while you're at it, I want you to find one for yourself as well. I can't have you driving around in that old car you've got now." I had one more perk for her. "And move into my place with me. It's right next door. There're two bedrooms."

"Are you kidding me?" she asked in awe.

"That's sort of how I felt when the Nash brothers gave me everything they did. But it's not a dream. We call them perks, and as long as you work for me, my perks are your perks." It felt good to share some of the good fortune I'd come into.

Stone came out of the kitchen with a tray of meats and cheeses. "I want you to bulk up on the protein, Sloan. I'm going to see to it that you gain back everything you've lost. Spinach wraps are in the oven. You need plenty of iron too. Stress can do a number on your body, and I'll make sure you eat only the best."

"You don't have to do that." I picked up a piece of thinly sliced turkey and bit into it. "But I do appreciate it, Stone. This is out of this world."

"I smoke my own meats," he said proudly. "And I know that I don't have to do this for you, but I want to do it. I care about you, Sloan. We all do."

Baldwyn sat across from me, and the smile in his eyes told me how happy he was to have me home. He could hardly take his eyes off me the entire time everyone was over. And when the last person left, leaving us alone, he came and sat next to me.

I'd had a dream about us just before I was woken up by Preston in my hospital room the night before. In the dream, my mother told me that Baldwyn was a trustworthy man and I should be incredibly careful about my decisions where he was concerned.

He just kept proving how much I meant to him too. Rescuing me, protecting me, and even taking care of me until I was able to take care of myself. It all showed me just how trustworthy he was.

Running his arm around my shoulders, he leaned in to kiss my cheek. "I could run a hot bath for you."

"Can we talk about something first?" I had to know how he felt.

I'd dropped some bombs on him back at the hospital and I wanted him to know that I'd spoken prematurely. I'd been afraid then. I was still worried about my judgment, but not where he was concerned.

"Sure, we can." He gave me his undivided attention.

"When I asked you to change my name ..."

He held up his hand, cutting me off. "I've already set that into motion. While the nurses were getting you ready to go this morning, I made a call to the attorney we worked with in Carthage. He can get your name changed back to your maiden name within the week."

I'd been joking, but now that it was going to happen, I was all for it. "Oh, thanks. That means a lot to me, Baldwyn." I'd only brough it up because I wanted to make sure he didn't think I was asking him to marry me in some very awkward way. Even if I had been.

"Not a problem." He got up, leaving me on the sofa. "I'll go get that bath going." He stopped then turned to look at me. "There's something I'd like to ask you."

"Shoot."

"Did you ask Delia to move in with you so you'd have someone there with you?" His expression was blank, so I wasn't sure why he wanted to know. "Because I think it's a great idea to have someone living with you."

I hadn't intended to even ask Delia to move in. It was a spur of the moment thing. I'd been contemplating staying with Baldwyn. But his words had me rethinking things.

Maybe I'd already fucked things up. Maybe he isn't interested in spending his life with a broken woman.

27

BALDWYN

JASPER GENTRY MET ME AT THE FINISHED BUILDING SIX MONTHS later. "The building is done." And that meant Sloan's job was over. It had been a week since we'd closed the contract with her and the other engineers.

We walked side by side through the empty rooms. "It looks great. Your team did an amazing job." Jasper shoved his hands into his pockets. "How're things with you and Sloan since her job has ended?"

"To be honest, I have no idea how things are with us. She and her personal assistant left the apartment last week. They're traveling around the hill country to find a place for Sloan to buy. She wants her own home." While I was proud of her and her accomplishments, I missed her. I'd missed her the whole time.

We never got back to us—not the real us. She had therapy to focus on. Her work to deal with. The investigation dealing with the body the cops found had ended only a week after Sloan and her father's ordeal. The body was her mother's, and she and her dad had to not only deal with that, but mourn her loss too. And I got left in limbo while she dealt with all that.

"That Preston guy is in jail still?" he asked.

"Awaiting trial, yeah." I didn't like how long it was taking to get that going. "He's sitting in county jail right now because the judge wouldn't grant him any bail. I should be happy with that, but I need more. He did the worst things to Sloan, and her mother and father. It bothers me sometimes that I didn't shoot him in the heart instead of the shoulder."

Jasper stopped walking to turn to me. "And what would that have accomplished, cousin?"

"He'd be dead." I knew that much. "And I'd feel better about Sloan's safety. I hate to give him credit for anything, but he did manage to take down an armed cop while under sedation and with a painful gunshot wound."

"Crazy people feel no pain," he offered. "But iron bars will keep him inside, where he belongs."

"People escape from jails and prisons all the time." I'd been researching how many escapes there had been from the facility Preston was in. "Only a few years ago an inmate escaped from the exact place Preston is now."

"Was he re-captured?" Jasper asked.

"He was. But it took them a week before someone reported seeing him in Houston. He'd made it from Austin to Houston, Jasper. Preston wouldn't bother trying to hide. He would just go straight for Sloan." I hated how my mind could get away from me. "Let's not talk about him. It makes my skin crawl."

"Mine too." He and I began walking again. "Have you lost interest in Sloan? Is that the problem?"

"She's lost interest in me." I never stopped loving her. "She got terribly busy right off the bat. She had her own personal stuff to deal with, plus the district attorney kept calling her in to give statements. She and her father had to make arrangements for her mother. And she took some time to stay with her dad while that was going on. It was hard on them both. They'd been thinking Audrey had run off with some man and each of them had some bad things they'd thought about her. To find out that she was killed for protecting her daughter brought up a lot of guilt."

"That is rough," Jasper agreed. "As busy as she was, did you try to make some time for just the two of you?"

"At first, yeah." Running my hand through my hair, I felt that old nagging sense of frustration I'd had since things went haywire. "She had her friend move into her place with her. That made it hard to get time alone with Sloan. In my opinion, she kept using the excuse of not wanting to leave her friend alone so she didn't have to spend time alone with me. She'd warned me that she might find herself not being able to trust people."

"In time, she might learn that she can trust you. If you don't give up on her." He put his hand on my shoulder as we went down the long hall that separated what would one day be hotel rooms for our guests. "Love is rare, cousin. It's not easy all the time either. But true love can withstand the hard times. It can even become stronger when you make it to the other side of those hard times."

"You know, I think I can make it to the other side. It's Sloan who worries me." I'd told our cousins all about what Preston had done. "The woman has some demons to slay. I'm just afraid that she thinks she has to slay them all before she can have a relationship with me."

"Do you think she feels broken by what's happened to her?" he asked. "She might feel like she's not enough for you. She might feel like you deserve someone who isn't messed up the way she is."

"I'm sure she does feel broken. And she most likely does think I deserve better. But she doesn't understand that I don't want anyone but her. Scars and all, I want her." No one else made me feel the way she did. And I felt sure that no one could ever take her place. "Preston broke something inside of me too.

He's as evil as they come. Sometimes I find myself praying that he rots in hell. I've never been that type of person who wishes ill on anyone. But that man made me into something akin to a monster myself. I dream about killing him sometimes."

"He hurt the woman you love. I would dream about killing him too if I were you. Have you thought about seeing a therapist, Baldwyn? It couldn't hurt."

"You're right. I'd thought about going to see one when this first happened. I don't know how that idea fell to the wayside. I know I was affected by what happened. Especially by how Sloan has pulled away from me." He was right. I did need help. "I'll never be the man she needs me to be if I don't get help."

"We all need help from time to time. There's nothing wrong with seeking it. It doesn't make you weak."

"I agree. I just forgot about getting any." I guess I had too many other things on my mind.

"You've been thinking about Sloan and not yourself." He smiled. "That is a sure sign of love."

I knew I loved Sloan; I just didn't know if she loved me. "And if she keeps putting space between us, then what should I do?"

"Sometimes our kids get between me and my wife. And sometimes the space between us is huge and lasts months. But I found out something that I'll share with you. See, they do go to sleep, eventually. Sometimes it's in our bed, separating us from each other. But what I figured out was that I can get up, pick up my wife out of that bed and take her down the hall to another room where we can reconnect without anyone in between us."

"Yeah, but she wants that too." I wasn't so sure that Sloan wanted to be alone with me. We hadn't been intimate in months. "The sex began to get a little rushed, then it lacked something. She blamed it on feeling disconnected from her own body. What was I supposed to do about something like that?"

"I suppose a therapist will let you in on that. I'm not saying I know how to make things work between you two again. I am saying that love is worth fighting for. I'm saying don't give up. Not yet. It's only been a few months."

"Half a year," I corrected him.

"Six months sounds better than half a year," he said as he mock punched me in the arm. "I'd love nothing more than to see you two back together and moving forward. The family needs more kids in it anyway."

"Oh, so now you want me to join the fatherhood circle too." I laughed, as I hadn't even thought about having kids. "I don't even know if Sloan wants kids."

I didn't care if we had babies or not. All I really cared about —for now—was that she would want me again. I wanted us to be us again. But I wasn't sure she would ever be the same person she'd been before she found out how much Preston had fucked with her.

"Do you think she can ever go back to who she was before all this happened to her?" I wasn't sure she could.

He shook his head, which made me feel hopeless. "You should know that people change all the time. My wife and I aren't the exact same people we were when we first met. I still love her. With the babies came differences in both of us. She became a mother and I a father. It wasn't just us anymore. We grew, evolved into different people. But the one thing that stayed true was our love for each other."

"So, what you're saying is that love is the constant in an ever-changing life. And Sloan and I had love. So, we have this lifeline for a relationship that we can use to make things work for us. But both of us have to want to make it work." I knew I couldn't do it all alone.

"Remind her of the bond you two share. Remind her of why you fell in love in the first place."

"I don't know how it happened. We were great friends in the first place." How it had all moved to something more eluded me.

"Are you still friends?" he asked with a grin.

"Yes. We talk at least three times a week and we talk for an hour or more each time." That was something, I supposed.

"Do you laugh together?"

"Yeah. She's pretty funny—even if she thinks she's all busted up inside. And we both know that I'm a riot." I could step it up. I could find ways for us to end up alone together without freaking her out. That's all we'd really need: to bring our friendship back to where it had been. The relationship would find its way back.

28

SLOAN

Sitting in the living room of my new home on Lake Travis, a short distance outside of Austin, I sipped my coffee while gazing out the wall of windows that looked over the lake. I'd only lived there a week but already it felt like home to me.

Although it was a bit on the lonely side, I loved everything about my new place. Delia opted to stay in the apartment, saying I needed to make this place mine and mine alone. It was time that I stopped using her as a crutch anyway.

I'd leaned on her far too much as it was. It was time to stand on my own two feet once again. Nine months of therapy had me understanding more about myself than I had even before all the horrible news came tumbling down on me.

The fact was that sometimes bad things happened to good people. It didn't make me or my mother stupid for being manipulated. We were simply trusting people who were taken advantage of by a terrible person.

For the longest time, I kicked myself repeatedly for being so damn stupid as to not see through Preston. I was done doing that to myself. And at least now I knew what to look for if anyone else tried to manipulate me.

It wouldn't be an easy task to take advantage of me anymore. But I didn't have to be afraid of other people. I didn't have to keep everyone at arm's length either.

"In other news, a man who was awaiting a trial date for murder, kidnapping, and attempted murder has committed suicide at the Travis County Correctional Center where he was incarcerated nine months ago," a female reporter said, drawing my attention to the television I'd turned on earlier.

"Preston," I whispered as I watched the screen.

His mugshot filled the screen as the reporter went on. "Preston Rivers hung himself in his quarters early this morning. His trial was scheduled for later this month."

I felt nothing at all. Not peace, not anguish, nothing. The doorbell rang and I turned to look at the front door. It was eight in the morning; I hadn't expected anyone to come over. I was still in my nightgown, but padded in bare feet to the door anyway to look out the peephole. "Baldwyn."

Opening the door, tears sprang up in my eyes for some reason. "I have something to tell you." He pulled me in, hugging me. "Preston's killed himself." His lips pressed against the top of my head.

"I know," I said as a sob came unexpectedly out of my mouth. "I just heard it on the news."

Sweeping me up into his strong arms, he carried me inside, kicking the door shut behind us. "I knew this would be hard on you. It's a shock, I know. And it's a let down too. I know you wanted him to stand trial and face what he did to you and your family."

I honestly had no idea why I was crying, and so hard at that. I couldn't even speak for all the crying I was doing. So many things swirled inside of me.

Part of me was mad that Preston had escaped being judged by a jury of his peers. Part of me was happy he wasn't walking the earth any longer. Part of me was sad because no matter how it all happened, I'd actually loved the man at one point. But the biggest part of me was elated—I was free of him for good. I would never have to see him in the flesh again for as long as I lived.

Baldwyn sat on a chair, holding me on his lap as he held me close, whispering, "It's going to be okay, baby. You're going to be fine. I'm with you. You're not alone in this."

He was right. Before he came, I didn't even know how to respond to what I'd just heard on the television. But as soon as I saw him, my emotions came crashing to the surface, insisting to be let out—set free.

Baldwyn was good for me. He was like a part of me in a way. He was the part of me that allowed me to express myself without fear that I would drown in my emotions.

It became crystal clear to me that I'd held everything back, buried it deep down, thinking all the pain would eventually go away on its own. Therapy had helped be come to that understanding, but it took a while for my mind to accept it. Pain, sorrow, fear, and even love don't just fade away in time. They have to be expressed, let go, set free.

I hadn't told Baldwyn that I loved him in a very long time. It was time he heard me say it again. "I love you so much, Baldwyn Nash. I know I've been elusive and haven't let you inside for a long time. I'm sorry."

"Don't be," he said, placing a kiss on the top of my head as I clung to him. "You needed the time to heal, Sloan. I've never been mad or upset with you even once all this time. I love you too. I always will."

Gulping back the sobs that rose in my throat, I wanted him to know something. I pulled my head off his chest to look at him through tear-filled eyes. "That time at the hospital when I asked you if you could change my last name—do you remember that?"

"I do." He smiled. "And I did that for you, Sloan Manning."

He hadn't understood what I wanted back then. "I was asking you to marry me. Albeit very clumsily."

His face froze as he looked at me. "You were?"

Nodding, I felt kind of stupid for mentioning it now. "I guess I was a little crazy at the time. And I'm glad you didn't catch on."

"Well, you didn't expand on what you said either. I think that was because the cops came into the room and your father was there. Your ex was lying on the floor as well. It was a little crowded in there." He gently pushed my hair away from my face. "It wasn't the right time for that. You were much too vulnerable then. I wouldn't have said yes anyway."

"And you would've been right to turn me down. I did have a lot going on." But I didn't have tons going on now. "I'm tired of being alone, Baldwyn."

"Me too." He kissed my cheek. "But I want to be sure you're okay. So, are you okay, Sloan?"

"I'm not perfect, but I don't think I ever will be. Mostly because perfection isn't real. We all have our scars. I'm not the only person in this world who has ever been dealt a shitty hand." I didn't know if I would ever be the same, but I did know that I wanted to be with Baldwyn. "I know we haven't spent much time together in the last nine months. And I'm probably a little different than I was before. But I'd like it if you could get to know the new me. You might like her, and you might not."

"I will like her," he said with a grin as he took me by the chin. "Wanna know why that is?"

"I would love to know why that is." My heart felt like it was blossoming inside my chest as he looked into my eyes.

"I love you, Sloan Manning. I love every part of you and every aspect of you. I want what's best for you and I know that's me. Your pain is mine. Your happiness is mine. We share more than you know." His lips touched mine, just barely.

I felt the charge of electricity as it built between us. He had to genuinely love me, or he wouldn't have waited around for me for so long. For the first time in a long time, I felt no fear. None at all.

Throwing my arms around him, I kissed him hard, needing to feel him in a way I hadn't in way too long. He kissed me back. His hands moved to caress my back and I ran my hands over his bulging biceps.

Standing up, he carried me to the sofa, laying me down and then covering me with his body. I moaned, delighted by the way his weight felt on me. I wanted more. Wrenching my mouth away from his, I found my voice husky as I asked, "Wanna take me to bed?"

He looked at me for what seemed like forever. "No." Moving off me, he left me feeling a little odd. I hadn't expected that answer.

Putting my arm over my face, I tried to hide the blush that came over me, feeling embarrassed for rushing things. Of course he didn't want to get right to having sex after we'd been on hiatus for nine months. *God, I'm an idiot!*

"I'm sorry, Baldwyn. I don't know what's gotten into me."

I felt his hands run up the front of my legs, then over my stomach before taking my hands, pulling me to sit up. "No need to be sorry. I just want to do something before we do anything else."

I'm sure he had questions before he let himself get vulnerable with me. "Do you want to know how my therapy has helped me?"

Shaking his head, he grinned. "No. I can see that's it's been doing you good. You look better and you seem to be having no trouble showing your emotions."

"What else could it be?"

"There's just this one question that I have." He let go of my hands and shoved them into his pockets. He was on his knees in front of me.

"Just one, huh?" I thought I knew what it was. Since we'd been sort of separated, I doubted that he'd brought any condoms. I'd never told him about me not being able to get pregnant. *Now might be the right time for that.*

He moved around, getting on one knee as he pulled his hands out of his pockets. In the palm of his right hand was a little black box. My heart stopped, my mouth went dry as a cotton ball, and I felt like I might pass out.

Opening the lid, he showed me what was inside. An absolutely gorgeous solitary diamond ring. "Sloan Manning, I've never known love, not true love, until I met you. You're the one and only woman for me. And I believe that I am the one and only man for you. I promise to cherish you, adore you, and love you for the rest of my life. Will you marry me?"

I did not expect this.

I put my hands over my mouth. My eyes went from his to the ring and they stayed there. He wanted to marry me. He wanted us to spend the rest of our lives together. Even though I was most likely hopelessly broken, he still loved me.

And I loved him all the more for it.

29

BALDWYN

WHEN YOU HAVE FOUR BROTHERS, YOU CAN'T PICK JUST ONE TO BE your best man. So, all my brothers stood with me at the altar as my best men. I couldn't marry my true love without them being a part of our wedding.

"Man, it's sort of scary up here," Stone mumbled. "I can't believe you're not running away, Baldwyn. I'm having to fight myself not to run. Aren't you afraid? I mean—this is it, bro. No more women for you. Just one. Sure, Sloan's a great one—the best. But no more flirting. No more touching other women. You've gotta be scared."

"Actually, I've never felt less afraid of anything. We've been through some tough stuff and through it all, my love for her has never faded even a little bit. This is right. I know it is." I shifted my weight to the other foot, as we'd been standing there a good ten minutes.

Patton craned his neck to try to see farther down the aisle than possible. "The preacher said she was ready. What's the hold up?"

Warner shot Patton a what-the-hell look. "Hey, man. Don't go giving Baldwyn any reasons to start freaking out. She's a little late is all. She's going to come down that aisle any minute. Sloan won't flake on him."

Flake on me?

I'd had no doubts. But now that the idea of Sloan changing her mind was brought up, I had many doubts. "She's been nervous as hell about this. She's changed her mind a hundred times about where she wanted the wedding, how many people she wanted here, and if she wanted a formal wedding at all. I thought she was settled on this small wedding with just a few of our friends here. But now I'm not so sure."

Cohen cleared his throat. "Don't let them get to you, bro. Sloan is definitely going to go through with this. She loves you."

"Yeah," I tried to calm myself down. "Yeah, she does." But she hates being the center of attention. "I should've just taken her to Vegas to do this. I shouldn't have told her that I wanted all you guys here for this. Maybe it's too much for her. Man, I've messed it all up."

Stone brough the preacher into the conversation, "Hey, preach, did the bride look nervous to you when you saw her?"

"She did." He nodded as he looked at me. "But they're always nervous. It's a nerve-wracking time, getting married. Even if you do it in Vegas."

"Yeah," Patton agreed. "But at least when you do it in Vegas, you can get screaming drunk beforehand. That would make it easier. This is brutal. We're all up here, waiting and waiting, while everyone just watches us squirm. I'm not going to do this. I can tell you that right now. If I ever get married, and that's a big if, because I like the ladies—all the ladies—I'm gonna do it Vegas style."

"Don't you want to be able to remember when you said your vows, Patton?" I asked him. "That's sort of an important memory. And the way you're talking, you'll be so shit-faced ..." I looked at the preacher, who frowned at me. "Pardon my French." I looked back at Patton as I went on, "You won't recall a thing about the best day of your life."

"Whoa, this is what you think is the best day of your life?" Stone asked with raised brows. "I thought that day when we went cliff diving was the best day of your life. You yelled that exact thing all the way down to the water."

"Come on, you guys." I couldn't believe any of them. "The best day of any man's life is when he gets married. Everyone knows that."

"Well, there are better days," the preacher interjected. "Like the day your children are born. Those are right up there too. And you'll be just as nervous then as you are now—maybe even more so."

Warner jabbed me in the ribs with his elbow as he stood next to me. "Babies, Baldwyn." One brow shot up. "Yikes!"

The mention of babies made a lightning bolt shoot through my head. "Shit!"

"It's not that bad," the preacher said. "Kids are lots of fun, Baldwyn."

"No, it's not that." I hadn't meant that I hadn't thought about having kids. "Sloan told me something last week." I knew she didn't want me saying anything about what she'd told me in confidence. So, I clamped my mouth shut.

All my bothers stared at me, waiting for me to say more. Cohen was the one to ask, "Well, what did she tell you?"

"I can't say." But I knew that had to be what was holding her up. "She must be worried that she won't make me happy, or I'll be disappointed in the future."

"And why would that happen?" Stone asked.

Because she thinks she can't have babies. Not that I was going to utter a word to anyone about that. "You know, people worry about disappointing other people all the time. And Sloan tends to worry a bit. But she'll never disappoint me—not ever."

"Well, don't put her up on such a high pedestal," the preacher said. "You will disappoint her, and she will disappoint you. We're all only human. We all disappoint at one time of another."

"I didn't mean it that way. I just mean that if she's worried about marrying me because of this thing we talked about, then she doesn't need to worry because I will never be disappointed about that." I knew I sounded looney, but I couldn't breathe a word about what she'd told me.

Something moving at the other end of the room caught my eye and I saw Delia waiting at the other end of the aisle, holding a bouquet of pink and yellow flowers.

The music started and my brothers and I lined back up. My heart pounded so hard I couldn't even hear the music. *Holy shit! Holy shit! Holy shit!*

Delia moved so slowly, that at times I thought she must be walking backward. The yellow chiffon dress hit her at the ankles, and it swirled around her silver sandaled feet with each step she took. My eyes were glued to the swirling action as my heart felt like it was about to explode out of my chest.

Finally, she took her place on the right side of the altar and then I heard the music change from the light twinkling music they'd picked for the maid of honor to walk down the aisle to. Sloan had chosen a song instead of the usual Wedding March.

One lone guitar played softly as the female singer began the song. "*It's amazing how you can speak right to my heart.*"

Sloan hadn't told me what song it was. And I hadn't heard this song in years. But it summed up how she felt about me perfectly. And I felt the same way about her. *You speak right to my heart too, baby.*

Sloan still hadn't come out yet and I found myself craning my neck to get a look at my bride as the singer went on. "*Without saying a word, you can light up the dark.*"

I just wanted Sloan to step out into the aisle and light up my world.

"*Try as I may, I could never explain what I hear when you don't say a thing.*"

Sloan was definitely making me wait, and the anticipation of seeing her in the wedding dress she'd given me no hints about was making me antsy.

And then there she was as the singer sang, "*The smile on your face lets me know that you need me.*"

I was beaming at her. I couldn't stop smiling. She looked utterly amazing in a flowing satin, bone-white wedding gown. It shimmered with each tiny step she took, a silver shoe peeking out from under the bottom of the dress each time.

"*The truth in your eyes says you'll never leave me.*"

I will never leave you, my love.

"*The touch of your hand says you'll catch me if I ever fall.*"

I will always catch you—you can count on me, my darling wife.

"*Now you say it best, when you say nothing at all,*" the singer tapered off, ending the song.

My bride took one final step, then she handed her bouquet to Delia before taking my hands. "Hi there, handsome. Wanna change my name now?"

"You bet I do." I wanted to kiss her so damn badly, but that part hadn't come yet. I had to wait. I had to be patient. "You look gorgeous."

Blushing, she ducked her head. "Thank you. I feel gorgeous."

"We are gathered here today," the preacher said, taking our attention. Perhaps he saw the need in my eyes to get to the good part, the part where I got to kiss my bride. "To join together this man and this woman in holy matrimony."

Her hands began shaking and I gave them a gentle squeeze to let her know that I was right here with her. We were doing this together, and she would never be alone again. Not as long as I had breath in my lungs and my heart had a beat left in it.

I couldn't tell you what else the preacher said that day. All I saw was Sloan, and all I felt was pure love for her. I knew that we'd be together forever, and I knew we'd weather more storms in our lives. But neither of us would have to weather any storm on our own. We'd be a team in every aspect. Sloan and I against the world.

Smiling up at me, she whispered, "You can kiss me now, hubby."

I'd gone through the motions, said yes when I was supposed to, and so had she. That was it, we were one. All that was left was to seal the deal with a kiss. "Can I?"

Nodding, her cheeks went pink as she pursed her lips. "You can."

I'd been in a rush to take those lips before, but now I just wanted to look at her. *Mrs. Nash.*

I looked back at my brothers to find them all with shining eyes. Patton even had a tear running down his cheek, which he quickly wiped away before anyone else could see it. "Thanks, brothers."

I turned back to look at my wife, who patiently waited for my kiss with closed eyes and puckered pink lips. I took her beautiful face in my hands then put my lips on hers. It wasn't a dominating kiss. It was equal on both sides. Her lips parted, allowing our tongues to dance as we made it official.

Everyone clapped as our kiss went on and on and on and I picked her up in my arms and walked down the aisle. "I present to you, Mr. and Mrs. Nash," the preacher shouted, and everyone cheered loudly.

The driver of the limo we'd rented held open the back door to the car and I slid my precious wife into the back seat. "Are you ready for this, Mrs. Nash?" I slid in beside her, holding her hand as the driver closed the door behind us.

"I'm ready if you are, Mr. Nash." Leaning in, she kissed me hard, then climbed over, straddling me.

This is gonna be some ride!

30

SLOAN

AFTER A TRADITIONAL WEDDING RECEPTION WITH CHAMPAGNE flowing like a waterfall, dancing to every song on both of our playlists, and eating more food than I'd ever eaten before, we staggered into our hotel room. "Well, that was something, wasn't it?"

"It was something," he agreed. "I loved it. But I *am* glad I never have to do that again."

"Me too." Baldwyn was it for me. I knew that without a doubt in the world. "I love this dress too, but I can't wait to take it off and never wear it again."

"Allow me." Baldwyn moved his finger in a swirling motion, gesturing for me to turn around.

"Thank you." I turned my back to him to let him unzip the dress. The zipper made a whizzing sound, then he pushed it off my shoulders and it landed in a heap around my feet.

His hands were warm on my back as he unhooked my bra, letting it fall to join the dress on the floor. His fingers grazed down my sides then he pushed down my white, silk panties. I stepped out of my heels, leaving everything behind, then turned to him, naked.

I reached out for his hand and he gave it to me. Leading him to the bed, I pushed him gently to get him to sit down. I took off one shiny black shoe and then the other. Sliding each black sock off, I ran my hands over his bare feet before moving them up to take his hands once again.

As I pulled him up, he leaned in for a kiss, which I had to deny him. "Not yet, hubby."

He'd gotten rid of the tuxedo jacket before we came to the room. All that was left was the white button-down shirt. I got to work unbuttoning it, then pulled it off him to reveal his chiseled torso.

Taking a moment to admire all the hard work he'd done on building that magnificent body, I ran my hands over his taut pecs, then down the ladder that separated his abs. My fingers played with the button on his pants, teasing him for a moment before I finished undoing it then slid my hands down his thick legs.

Bent over, I faced the massive erection that hid behind his black boxer briefs. I couldn't let him be so uncomfortable, so I got rid of the undies, leaving him just as bare as I was. "There we are—equal."

He nodded. "That we are." Lifting his hands, he took the bobby pins out of my fancy updo one by one, allowing my hair to cascade down in silky waves. I'd let it grow and it hung to my waist. "You were gorgeous in your dress, with your hair all fixed up. And you're still gorgeous with nothing on and your hair down. You're like a little miracle, aren't you?" he asked with a grin.

"Nah." I was just a woman who loved her man.

He took my hand, then pulled me onto the bed with him. Leaning up on one elbow, he looked at me, playing with a lock of my hair, twirling it around his finger. "I'm not gonna lie, I'm exhausted. I bet you are too."

"Wiped out," I confirmed. "But not too tired to consummate our marriage."

"Then consummate we shall, my love." He ran his hand along one side of my face as he moved in for a kiss.

We'd kissed off and on all night long. But this kiss was different. It wasn't even the same type of kiss we'd shared at the altar. This kiss made my head spin, my toes curl, and my heart race. This was the first kiss before sex as a married couple—and this kiss was hot!

Gripping his wrist, I arched my body up, needing to feel him inside of me with an intensity I'd never experienced before. He moved his hand away from my face, trailing his fingers along my neck, then over my breast before moving it down my stomach. Playing with my clit, he made sure it was plump and swollen before he spread my legs open and moved his body between them.

Panting with excitement, I yearned to have him inside of me. When he pushed his hard erection into my wet tunnel, I whimpered with ecstasy. "Yes."

He moved slowly, pushing in, pulling out, undulating as he watched me. "God, you are beautiful."

Reaching up to him, I ran my hands over his muscular chest as he kept moving, making long and deep strokes. "I think you're beautiful too." I ran my hands through his thick curls, loving the manly scent that escaped them.

"Aww, you're sweet." He kissed the tip of my nose, making me smile.

"So are you." I pulled him down to me so I could kiss him, wrapping my legs around him, making him go even deeper into me.

I wasn't sure if I would ever tell him how scared I'd been to walk down that aisle and make vows that would join us forever.

Not because I had any doubts about him being a wonderful husband, but I had doubts about myself.

I'd finally told him about me not being able to have children about a week before the wedding. He didn't even blink an eye as he'd said, "I love you and all that comes with you. If we have kids, great. If we don't, that's great too. All that really matters is that I get to spend my life with you."

I wasn't sure if he was being honest with himself when he'd said those things.

As I waited in the dressing room, looking at myself in the full-length mirror, wearing my wedding dress, I worried that someday Baldwyn would be disappointed that he would never get to be a father. He would never know the joy of holding his first-born, look into their tiny eyes and see a part of himself there. I almost left. I almost walked right out of there. I didn't want to keep the man I loved from having that.

But as I hitched up my dress to make a mad dash out of there, my mother's voice came out of nowhere, "You have nothing to fear, my dear."

I wasn't sure I'd really heard her. "Mom?"

Apparently, ghostly voices don't repeat themselves. I didn't hear another word. But what I had heard stuck in my mind. And for some reason, I felt fine again. That's when I grabbed my bouquet of flowers and went to meet my fiancé.

Baldwyn's mouth left mine, then he kissed a line down my neck before nipping my earlobe.

I ran my foot along the back of his thigh as a moan escaped me. "Harder, babe."

Moving faster, he put his hands on either side of me and raised his upper body off mine so he could do as I asked. "Harder, huh?" Slamming into me, he gave me what I wanted.

My nails bit into the flesh on his arms as I held tightly to his biceps to keep from being moved up the bed by his powerful thrusts. "Yes! Oh, God, yes!" The wave began to build up, welling from deep inside of me.

"Give it to me!" he barked as he pounded me. "I want it all."

"Ahhhh," I screamed as I came undone.

My canal pulsed around his cock, urging him to release as well. He did so with an enormous growl that shook us both. Gasping for air, he fell on top of me, his cock throbbing inside of me as he gave me all he had to give.

Feeling completely satisfied, I ran my hands over his back as we both fell asleep, staying connected. Being connected to him made me feel whole in a way I couldn't feel without him.

So, this is what people mean when they call their spouse their better half.

I couldn't have wished for a better man to share my life with. I had to wonder though, that if this came true for me, then maybe something I'd actually wished for could come true too.

My sixth-birthday wish was the only I really remembered. A pony was all I'd wished for that year. *Can one become too grown up to own a pony?*

31

EPILOGUE
BALDWYN

3 MONTHS LATER...

The grand opening of Whispers Resort and Spa had come. Everyone had dressed to the nines and we were all excited. I held up my glass of champagne to make a toast. "To everyone who helped my brothers and I see our dream come to fruition."

"Cheers!" everyone called out as we all clanked our glasses together.

The place was gorgeous, and I was sure it would be a great success.

Sloan was sure of it too. "You're all going to do great, Baldwyn. I'm so proud of you."

She went to kiss my cheek, but I turned my face and got a nice one right on the lips. "You're a part of this too, you know. Now you're not only a successful structural engineer, you're part-owner of this place."

"Look at me." She laughed as she put her glass of champagne down on a table, having not taken even a sip of it. "From pauper to part-owner of a fancy resort and spa. Who would've ever thought this would happen to a girl like me?"

All joking aside, she'd been destined for greatness all along.

"You don't like the Armand de Brignac?" At nearly ten thousand bucks a bottle, I would think everyone would enjoy the champagne. "It's pink, you're favorite color."

"I'm sure it's delicious," she said with a smile. "I'm not thirsty right now."

"K, babe." I wrapped my arm around her waist then kissed the side of her head. "You seem tired. We don't have to stay late."

"No, I'm fine. We can stay as long as you'd like. This is a big day for you and your family. I don't want to spoil it for any of you." She spotted her assistant and friend, Delia, coming in and excused herself. "I'm going to say hi to Delia. Go hobnob."

Something wasn't right about Sloan. She was acting very weird. I'd heard her on the phone before we'd left the house. When she'd seen, she ended the call without even saying good-bye. And when I'd asked her who it was, she said nobody.

Her father, Richard, came in from the back way. I met him, handing him her glass of champagne since she hadn't touched it. "Thanks for coming, Richard."

He took a drink and raised his brows. "This is amazing."

"It ought to be." I hadn't thanked him yet. "By the way, thanks for giving me the great advice about giving Sloan a pony for a wedding present. She loves it. I swear she'd keep it in our bedroom if I hadn't had an adorable barn built for it to live in."

"She told me about it." He laughed. "She said that she knew wishes could come true now since she'd never told anyone about her childhood birthday wish. I guess she didn't recall telling me and her mother about what she was going to wish for the day before she turned six."

"Ha!" I had no idea she thought that way about the present. "I never mentioned to her that you'd given me the idea either. What a hoot that woman is, believing wishes can come true. She's adorable."

"Well, I hope she's not completely wrong about that. I've

been wishing for something for you both since your wedding day. I won't say what it is, or it might not come true." He held up his glass. "To wishes coming true."

I touched my glass to his, unsure what he was talking about, but when someone is talking about wishes coming true, it just seems like something I should agree with. "To wishes coming true. Cheers."

"Cheers," he echoed.

I watched Sloan as she and Delia talked only to each other before leaving the room. The large lobby served as our party room. I had high hopes of seeing it filled with guests the following day. We already had loads of reservations.

Going around the room, I chatted it up with our cousins and their wives, who'd all flown in for the party. And then I saw Sloan coming out of the hallway, rushing to me with a huge smile on her face.

She was waving a pen in the air, almost hopping up and down as she came running up to me. "Baldwyn, we did it!"

"Did what?" I grabbed her hand to find out what was so exciting about this pen she had. "And what's it got to do with this pen?"

"It's not a pen." She let me have the pink stick, a look of confusion on my face. I had no idea what I was looking at. "It's a pregnancy test. And it's positive." She threw her arms around my neck as she squealed with joy, "We're going to have a baby!"

"A baby?" *I thought she couldn't have children.* "Are you sure about this, Sloan?" I didn't want to get my hopes up.

But it seemed she had. "Yes! I'm positive now that I've taken the test. I think I'm about three months pregnant. You're gonna be a daddy. I'm gonna be a momma! A mother! Oh my God!"

I looked at her father, who couldn't wipe the smile off his face. My brothers and cousins came up, patting me on the back and offering their congratulations. But I wasn't sure this was real.

She said she couldn't have kids. This can't be real.

Suddenly her father was there with us, hugging his daughter. "Wishes really can come true. I've been wishing this for you two since your wedding day."

Wishes can come true?

Sloan: 6 months later …

I held our daughter in my arms only moments after she came into the world, screaming her tiny head off. "Hi there, pretty girl. Your momma loves you very much."

Baldwyn leaned in, running his hand over her head. "So does your daddy." He kissed me on top of the head. "She's as pretty as her momma."

"Prettier," I whispered.

I'd been so worried about not being able to have children. But I hadn't ever gotten checked out to find out why I never had them with Preston. I suppose God didn't want me to have children with that monster.

Whatever God's reasoning was for those childless years, I didn't care. Baldwyn and I had a baby. We had a perfect little girl to call our own. And the doctor had found nothing wrong with my reproductive organs to stop us from having as many babies as we wanted.

Of course, I wasn't ready to even think about having another baby. But in the future, I could think about it. That meant a lot to me and I knew it meant a lot to Baldwyn too.

"We're going to have to decide on her name," he said as the nurse came to take her away so the doctor could check her out.

I didn't want to let her go, but finally did. "Hurry back, little angel."

Baldwyn and I had a hard time sticking with a name. We'd gone from cute names like Brie and Tulip to romantic names like Anastasia and Millicent. We even looked up Biblical names like Sarah and Mary. But they all lacked in some way or another.

Baldwyn took my hand, kissing it as he gazed at me. "We've thought of every name in the word, but none have seemed to fit. And now that I've seen her, I think I've got the perfect name for her."

"Me too." The name had jumped into my brain as soon as I laid eyes on her. "We're often on the same page. Should we just say it together and see what we have?"

He looked a little worried, his brow furrowed. "I don't want to drown you out with what I say. How about we write it down and exchange papers?" He looked around and found a little notepad and a pen.

I liked the idea. "If we have different names, let's just make a compromise and pick one for the first name and one for the middle name."

"Sounds fair to me." He handed me the pen and paper. "By the way, I know I keep telling you how proud I am of you. But, baby, I am really proud of you. You are some sort of a superhero. I can't imagine doing what you just did. And carrying the baby for nine months too—growing her inside of your body! Wow! Just—wow!"

"Aw, shucks, weren't nothin'—almost anyone can do it. Well, anyone with a uterus that is." I wrote the name down then pulled the sheet of paper off, folding it up so he couldn't see what I'd written. Handing the pen and pad of paper back to him, I added, "But thank you for appreciating all my hard work."

"Not a problem. I'm going to rock as a daddy." He wrote down his name, then pulled the sheet off, folding it up.

Our daughter cried and we both looked over at her. The doctor had poked her little heel, making her cry. "Why'd you do that?" I asked with an angry expression.

"We need a little bit of blood to do a PKU test. It's a rare disorder that can lead to brain damage if not treated in infancy." The nurse swaddled our baby up again then brought her to me.

"Sorry about making your little angel cry. It's necessary though. As parents, you should know that there will be shots and other things that will make your baby cry. But they are all to keep her healthy. Being a parent is hard sometimes." She shrugged. "Lots of times. But there are far more awesome times than hard times. So, there's that. What are we to call this young lady?"

Baldwyn handed me his paper and I handed him mine. "We're about to find out," I told her.

Unfolding the page, I closed my eyes, not wanting to be disappointed if the name he picked wasn't my cup of tea. "Well, here it goes." I opened my eyes and had to blink. "Wow."

Baldwyn opened the paper I'd written on and looked back at me. "Wow, babe."

"Can you believe this?" I held out the paper to the nurse and Baldwyn did too.

She read the names we'd both chosen out loud. "Audrey Rose. I like it."

"Audrey was my mother's name." I couldn't stop smiling at my husband.

"And Rose was my mother's name," Baldwyn said. "It fits our little girl well, doesn't it?"

"Yes, it does," I agreed as I took our baby back into my arms.

It might have taken a bit and we might have gone through some tough times, but we made it. Baldwyn and I had found it, our happily ever after.

The End

www.ingramcontent.com/pod-product-compliance
Lightning Source LLC
Chambersburg PA
CBHW071029160225
22036CB00028B/675